Harley's Achilles
Sandrine Gasq-Dion

Dedication

First and foremost, to my loyal readers, bloggers, and reviewers. I love you all. I would not be where I am without you.

Michael Stokes for being my friend and taking fabulous pictures.

Zack Hardt and Robert England for coming out to Sedona, AZ for me and looking fabulous.

Michelle Muhlbeier for the naughty, naked spider monkey.

Jenjo

Heidi Ryan

Ann Lister for sharing her Rock Gods with me and making me laugh on a daily basis.

Kellie Dennis for the cover.

Tyler and the guys at the Green Room.

Aarin, James, and Doug.

Achilles

2 months earlier
Universal Studios, CA

"Dammit! Where the fuck did he go?" I ran a hand through my hair and let out an exasperated sigh. Somehow, Harley had gotten away from me again. One minute I was in his bathroom, the next, Harley was gone and he'd left his clothing on the bed. Now I was worried he was running around the hotel naked.

"Fuck," Jinx sighed next to me. "We'll split up? Maybe we'll find him faster that way."

"Okay." I'd called Jinx the minute I realized Harley wasn't in the room anymore. I was trying to keep him from drinking too much at the bar, but he was a slippery little shit.

We split up and I cased the bar again and then headed down to the lobby. Still no Harley. I crossed the hotel to the pool area and stepped through the gate. The pool lights were on and the hot tub was bubbling.

"Achilles?"

I turned my head to see Jayden Dempsey relaxing in the hot tub.

"You didn't happen to see a half-naked Harley run by, did you?" I asked.

"That was Harley?" Jayden said in astonishment.

"Don't tell him where I am!" Harley whispered loudly.

I exhaled in complete frustration and advanced on the lounge chairs. Harley darted out and I caught him easily.

"Let me go, ya big asshole!" Harley struggled in my grip.

"Okay." I dropped Harley in the pool.

A pissed off Harley broke the surface, spitting water.

"Dammit! It's cold! My buzz is gone!" Harley shouted.

"Get out of the pool, Harley," I instructed quietly.

"Come and get me!" Harley crossed his arms and stared at me with an exaggerated pout.

Soft laughter met my ears and I turned to see Jayden at my side. He was trying to cover up his fit of laughter with his hand. I turned to him and cocked a brow.

"You want to join him?" I asked.

"Nope." Jayden shook his head.

"If I have to come get you, Harley, it's going to be a long night." I folded my arms across my chest and glared at a shivering Harley in the pool.

"Fine!" Harley swam to the stairs and wobbled out of the pool. I strode over and grabbed a towel out of a nearby cabinet. I wrapped Harley up, rubbing his arms.

"There you are!" Jinx yelled as he entered the pool area. He stopped mid-stride when he noticed Jayden. "What are you doing out here?"

"I'm sorry, that's your business why?" Jayden snapped.

I looked from Jayden to Jinx, and then to Harley. I put my arm around Harley's shoulders and began walking.

"Night, Jinx," I called out over my shoulder.

"Make sure he drinks water," Jinx said.

I gave him a thumbs up and walked Harley back to his room. He was shivering, his teeth chattering so loud I thought they'd break. I opened his hotel room door and ushered him inside. Harley leaned against the wall, his buzz not quite gone completely.

"Achilles," Harley slurred.

"Yes?" I grabbed a towel from the bathroom and then stood in front of him.

"I'm not a baby," Harley pouted.

"You need to get in the shower, you've got goose bumps all over you and your teeth are chattering. Do I have to put you in there?"

"Nah, I'll get in." Harley threw the towel off and shoved his Speedos down to his ankles. He jerked around trying to get them off his ankles and then kicked them across the room. My eyes traveled south and that was when I got a good look at Harley's dick. I almost swallowed my tongue. My head snapped up and I kept my eyes on his face as I tried to help him into the bathroom.

"You're so tall," Harley said as he stood in front of me. "And you have huge arms. Do you have huge feet, too?"

"I'm not sure what huge is, Harley." I tried to maneuver him into the bathroom.

"You have to know how sexy you are. You know that, right?" Harley ran a hand down my chest and I backed up a bit.

"What did you drink tonight, Harley?" I asked as I pushed him into the shower.

"Don't know."

I leaned forward to turn on the water and Harley yanked me into him by my shirt. His lips crashed into mine, and then his arms wrapped around my neck. God help me, half of me wanted to devour him, and the other half...well, it wanted to devour him. In seconds, Harley had shimmied up my body and attached himself to me like a naughty, naked spider monkey. His teeth nipped at my lips until I opened up, and then he plunged his hot tongue into my mouth. I went from zero to sixty in one second, giving Harley as good as I was getting. A feral growl rose within me and I pinned Harley to the wall, ravishing his mouth. Our tongues dueled and moans reverberated around the bathroom as we went at each other like horny teenagers. My brain finally caught up with my mouth and I untangled myself from him. I couldn't catch my breath and my dick was like iron in my pants.

"Harley? What the hell?" I croaked.

"Ooops." Harley grinned. "I just wanted a taste."

As soon as those words left his mouth, Harley was jumping out of the shower and lunged towards the toilet. I held him as he threw up again and again until there was nothing left but bile. I got him showered, and then I called room service and had them bring some ginger ale while I put Harley to bed.

"Here, sip a little more for me." I held the cup against his lips.

"It's warm." Harley's nose twitched.

"Just sip."

Harley did as he was told, and then lay back in bed. I made sure he was covered and then placed a wastebasket next to the bed. His eyelids drooped and he sighed heavily.

"Feeling better?" I asked.

"Are you going to stand at the end of the bed all night?" Harley opened his eyes and stared at me.

"Yes. I am."

"How come?"

"Because I'm worried about you."

"You'd be the only one." Harley sighed and closed his eyes again.

"You know that's not true," I said quietly.

Harley was out cold, softly snoring. I sat on the edge of the bed and pushed his hair off his face. I'd been with the Skull Blasters band for a few months and had gotten to know each of the members pretty damn well, but Harley was a whole different story. He stood out from the rest of them from the second I met him. He was hurting on the inside, and for the first time in a long time, I was starting to have feelings. I sat for hours just watching him. I couldn't help it. Harley whimpered in his sleep and tossed from side to side. I crawled in next to him and pulled him into my chest. He settled down immediately, snuggling into me.

Oh, this was so bad.

Chapter 1
Present day
Harley

The TV was blasting in the living room as I headed into the kitchen with the groceries I'd just bought for my parents. They were watching *Wheel of Fortune* or something like that. Neither one even acknowledged my presence as I walked right by them. Nothing new there. I could bring in the whole marching band from the school, along with a herd of elephants, and they wouldn't bat an eyelash. I put the stuff away and then headed upstairs. I faltered on the last step as I noticed my older brother's bedroom door was slightly ajar. That never happened; his room was a shrine. I took that last step and crossed to his door, opening it the rest of the way. Nothing was moved, everything was still in its place. My mother dusted in there every week and put everything back right where it had been, just in case he came home.

He wasn't coming back home. Not ever, because Holden Payne had been killed in Afghanistan.

My heart ached as I ran my fingers across his desk. The picture of the two of us astride his Harley motorcycle was still sitting there. God, I missed Holden. Not that my parents had paid me any mind before he passed away. I had been the surprise. Even after my father's vasectomy, I still made it through. Holden had made things ... tolerable. We used to do stuff together. He took me places and always doted on me because he knew my parents didn't even know I was alive. Should I have hated him for being their favorite? Maybe, but I didn't. Holden was my mom *and* my dad blended into one.

Now I just felt alone.

I shut his door behind me as I left, and then wandered into my old room, which was now the sewing/workout room. Amazing how I paid off the house for my parents, paid their bills and bought the groceries, but I didn't rate my own room.

Oh, that was right. I didn't exist.

I'd moved out right after Holden died. Why stay? He wasn't there anymore, and as much as I tried to convince my parents to move, to get away from the memories, they declined. I headed back to the living room. My parents were still watching their show. Pictures of Holden were scattered all over the room, from his childhood to his Army portrait. A neatly folded American flag in its oak case graced our fireplace mantel. Holden was everywhere, and I had to get out.

"Okay, I'm headed back to my house," I said as loudly as I could.

I got a slight wave of my father's hand, and that was it.

I hung my head and grabbed my jacket and keys off the table by the front door. It was almost Christmas and I was going to spend it with my Skull Blasters bandmates: Ransom Fox, his brother, Gareth Wolf, and Rebel Stryker. Oh, and with the bane of my existence -Achilles, the bodyguard from hell.

I was really missing Jinx Jett right now, but he was off with his boyfriend, Jayden Dempsey, on the London Boys tour. Jinx was our drummer, and a former man-whore. He'd met Jayden for the first time at a mall and had given him an autograph. The second time? Well, that story was a lot more interesting. They had met at a gay bar when Jinx had been trying out a glory hole for the first time. He had worked up the nerve to put his dick in. Jayden had been the receiver of said dick. The third time they met had been the clincher. Jayden was part of London Boys, a boy band, and Jinx totally hated boy bands. However, after spending two weeks together in California, Jinx and Jayden had gotten closer. Now they were in love.

I was happy for my best friend, don't get me wrong, but I missed him in my life. Jinx called a lot, and we Skyped, but there was a void in my life now. I stepped out into the garage and stopped in front of Holden's motorcycle. He and my dad had a thing for Harleys, so here I was, Harley James Payne. I'd tried to take the bike out and that was about the only time my father said anything to me. He screamed at me not to touch it.

Holden would have hated it, his bike gathering dust three years after his death. He would want me to ride it, he'd want me to take it on the curves in Camp Verde and Black Canyon. I touched the chrome and smiled. We'd had good times on the bike, he and I. I pushed the memories aside and walked out into the driveway. There, perched on the hood of my truck, was Achilles. I cursed and he jumped off the hood, striding over to me in two steps. Damn, the man was tall.

"Harley." Achilles stood over me.

"You know, I *hate* that tone of voice." I looked up at him. "I'm not a child."

"Then stop acting like one."

"How did you find me this time?" I folded my arms across my chest and gazed up at him. Achilles was what I would call an Adonis. He belonged in an art museum. His chiseled jawline and straight nose complemented his high cheekbones. His eyes, on the other hand   well, they were hard to describe. They reminded me of blue quartzite, but there was some gray in there with a little …

"I'm former Special Forces, Harley. I can find a needle in a haystack."

"Well, that would take time, now wouldn't it?"

"Yes, but you seem to think you're Harry Potter." I blinked. "Huh?"

"Get this through your thick skull, Harley. I'm not leaving your side."

Why did that thrill me *and* annoy me?

"Even if I had a pocketful of fucks, I still wouldn't give you one," I tossed flippantly over my shoulder as I approached my truck. A strong hand gripped my bicep, and then I was a hair's breadth from Achilles' face.

"Don't ever think you can shake me, Harley Payne. You got that? And drive slower! Are you trying to kill yourself?"

"Yes, Achilles," I agreed wryly.

"It's not funny." Achilles leaned even closer to me, and my hair stood up on the back of my neck. "I'm responsible for you; do you know what that means?"

"Is it that Chinese proverb thingie?"

"No." Achilles sighed, rubbing his face with his hands.

Jesus, the guy's biceps were bigger than my thighs. He could probably break a brick with his thighs, come to think of it …

"Harley!"

"Wha?!"

"Are you listening to me?"

"Yup."

I was trying, though. Achilles searched my eyes, and I swear sweat dripped down my back. What was it about this guy that set me on edge? His hand rose and hovered by my face. The wind rustled the trees and Achilles blinked and stepped back from me.

"Go home, Harley," he instructed as he walked down the driveway.

"Should I set a place for you at the dinner table?" I called out to him jokingly.

Achilles stopped and looked over his shoulder. "Yes. You should."

I started at that. Achilles didn't come in my house. At least, I didn't think he did. What did I know? He'd probably painted himself onto my wall like Rambo did in the movie with mud.

"French fries or tater tots?" I tried to keep it light, even though I was shitting my pants.

"Neither. Baked potato. And don't worry, I'll get the groceries."

"How do you know I have potatoes?"

"In the pantry, bottom shelf."

"Ah ha!" I pointed. "You *have* been in my house."

Achilles walked back to me and leaned into my face. "I am everywhere, Harley. Don't forget it."

I stood there and stared as Achilles walked away again. Why did that man infuriate me so much?

And why was I staring at his ass?

I knew why.

I'd had a threesome back in the day with a chick and her boyfriend. I had kissed the guy and we had crossed swords once or twice, but I hadn't gotten fucked. I did, however, fuck *both* of them. Too much tequila was to blame for that night. I was still staring at Achilles' ass as it got further away. Something about that man just made me want to wrestle him. Naked.

I jumped in my truck and drove back to my house with Holden and my parents still on my mind. I'd tried over the last three years to get them out of the house and into the sun, but they were content to sit and wait for Holden. It was as if they didn't believe he was gone, even though he was buried right here in town and they went to his funeral. I was so grateful the guys had been there with me the day of the funeral. If they hadn't been, I would have stood there alone.

I was always alone.

I knew that sounded stupid, considering people constantly surrounded me, but a part of me has always felt, well, invisible. I pulled into my driveway and waited for the garage door to open before sliding my baby inside. Holden always wanted a Ford F250 diesel, so I got one. She was black with flames down the side, and his name was among those flames. I stepped into the foyer of my house and shivered. It really was cold out. I checked the thermostat and inched it up a few degrees. I stepped into my living room and grabbed some firewood, throwing it into the fireplace and lighting it up. I loved my fireplace. Jinx and I always made s'mores during the winter.

I walked over to the picture on the wall of the guys and me. We were all smiling and flipping off the camera. It seemed weird that we all stayed so close. Most people who formed friendships in elementary school didn't stay as close as we did. We were always together; me, Paul, Ransom, Rebel, Jinx and Gareth. I ran my finger over Paul's face in the photograph. He was doing better, but he still had a long way to go. When Gareth was getting threatening notes, never in our wildest dreams did we think it could be Paul could be behind them. Turned out, Paul was jealous of Gareth and wanted to come back as our lead guitarist. We'd since been informed that Paul had chronic depression and PTSD, which played a huge role in his behavior. He was getting help now, and we hoped to bring him back to Arizona soon.

I sighed and walked into the kitchen. I didn't really cook. Most of my meals were the frozen kind or the pizza delivery kind, but once in a while, I liked a steak on the grill. I opened the pantry and smiled at the potato bag on the bottom shelf.

Damn Achilles.

When we were told we'd have a security detail, I thought it was only during tours. Turns out it was all the time, and my lucky ass wound up with brooding Achilles. I pulled the potatoes out and wrapped them in foil. I stepped out onto the patio and immediately shivered. Was I nuts grilling in December? I lit the grill and threw the potatoes on. I shut the sliding glass door and wandered back into the kitchen. The doorbell rang and I crossed the living room to answer it. I had barely gotten to the knob when the door flew open, revealing Achilles loaded down with bags.

"Why do you even bother to use the doorbell if you're just going to walk in?" I stood with my hands on my hips and what I hoped was a scowl on my face.

"You took too long," Achilles answered, shoving two bags into my arms.

I followed him back to the kitchen and placed my bags on the counter, rifling through them. I grinned as I spotted marshmallows and chocolate. I knew Jinx and Achilles talked a lot, which was probably why Achilles knew so much about me. Achilles pulled out a box of graham crackers and I turned to face him.

"Making s'mores?" I asked hopefully.

"Yes. We are," Achilles replied.

"Have you ever had them?" I asked, curious. I knew he'd been in the military before becoming a bodyguard. I had always wondered what those guys did during downtime. If they even had any.

"No. We spent most of our time telling ghost stories around the fire and singing," Achilles said with a straight face.

I narrowed my eyes. "You're fucking with me, right?"

"Yes. I am. We did have something along those lines," he told me as he pointed to the chocolate and marshmallows. "But they weren't the same. M.R.E.'s can only do so much."

"M.R.E's? I think my brother mentioned them once. Meals ready to eat. I hear they give you the shits."

"Among other things." Achilles placed the groceries on the counter and glanced at me. "Grill on?"

"Yep."

"I'll go put these steaks on."

Achilles seemed at ease in my kitchen, which again made me wonder how many times he'd been in my house. I made salad to keep busy and peeked out the glass door now and then to watch Achilles. His mother had definitely named him correctly. He was tall, and I mean, like really *tall*. I topped out at six foot, but Achilles towered over me. I checked out the curves of his ass as he bent over, and whistled softly under my breath. Achilles straightened and then turned around, and I quickly went back to work chopping tomatoes.

What was it about Achilles that turned me on so damned much? I'd always considered myself straight with a side of bi, but Achilles? Well, he turned my head so fast, I think I got whiplash the first time I laid eyes on him. And now he was in my fucking space 24/7. He was disgustingly good looking, but the side of him I liked the most was how he could be so caring and sweet. I rinsed my hands in the sink as Achilles came through the back door with the steaks. He placed the platter on the counter and handed me a knife.

"Do they look done?" he asked.

I cut one of the thicker ones in the middle and took a peek at the meat. "Yup, nice and pink."

"The potatoes have a few more minutes, I think. I can squish them, but not too much."

"Squish them, eh?" I grinned.

"You know what I mean." Achilles chuckled.

I jumped up on the counter and swung my feet out. "Do you even like hanging around me?"

"Well, you're never boring, that's for sure. You keep me on my toes."

"Do you like your job?" I picked up a carrot and munched on the end.

"Yeah. I mean, the hours are weird, but the paycheck is good and I get to see different places."

"I always wanted to travel when I was younger. Holden and I—" I stopped and swallowed hard.

"You and Holden what? Tell me." Achilles leaned against the counter.

"We were both going to join the military. I mean, I wanted to, but he begged me not to."

"Why?"

"Because he said he couldn't stand it if something happened to me," I said softly.

"But something happened to him." Achilles lifted my chin with his fingers and searched my eyes.

"Yes," I nodded. "Why did you join?"

"I wanted to see the world."

Achilles removed his fingers from my chin and stepped back. He jerked his chin toward the sliding glass door.

"I'm going to check the potatoes."

I stared at him. That was the first time Achilles had ever touched me like that. I didn't know if he knew it or not, but he almost touched my face today at my parents' house. I was almost positive he wasn't gay. I think. He looked older than me, too. I wondered how *much* older.

He brought in the potatoes, and we sat at my little kitchen table and ate. It felt weird to be sitting there with him, although, I had to admit I enjoyed the company. I wanted to know more about him, but was afraid to push too hard. Achilles seemed a little closed off.

"So, how's the album coming along?" The question startled me out of my thoughts.

"Really good. We've got twelve tracks completely done and when Jinx comes back, we can finish the rest."

"You miss Jinx, don't you?"

"Yeah. I'm happy for him though. He had it rough in school."

"What about you?" Achilles asked as he spread butter on his potato.

"I didn't have a problem with the ladies." I shrugged. "I guess I have charisma," I smirked.

"You have something, all right." Achilles basically snorted, and that made me laugh.

"I know, I'm a pain in the ass." I leaned back in my chair and let out a sigh.

"No, I wouldn't say pain in the ass. You are…adventurous?"

"Pain in the ass." I pointed at him with my fork.

"Thrill seeking?"

"Nice way of saying pain in the ass."

Achilles chuckled. "You are something else, Harley Payne."

I tilted my head. "How did you get here? I always see you, but don't see what you drive."

"Well, tonight I've come in my pickup truck. Normally, I'm on my Tomahawk."

My mouth fell open. "Excuse me? Dodge Tomahawk?"

"One and the same." Achilles nodded.

"Well, fuck. No wonder you catch me all the time. How fast does that go? Four hundred?"

"Four-twenty. Zero to sixty in two point five seconds."

"Fuuuckkkk. I think I just came."

Achilles cracked up and I smiled. I loved the sound of his laugh. Rich and hearty.

"Do you think I could ride it sometime?" I asked with a grin.

"I'll take you for a spin tomorrow if you want."

"I would. I miss being on a motorcycle."

"Why don't you buy one? Rebel has one."

"Because the one I want, I can't have." I stood, grabbing my plate from the table. "Are you finished?"

"I am, but I can get my own plate, Harley."

I took my dish to the sink and ran the hot water. Achilles joined me and placed his plate on top of mine. The heat from his body seemed to fill the air and I inhaled his intoxicating scent.

"Um, do you think you could stay? I mean, here...tonight?"

"Sure." Achilles nodded. "Let me just grab my bag from the truck."

"You packed a bag?"

"I always have an emergency go bag in my truck. Clothes, food, water, all the things you'd need if you were stuck." Achilles motioned to the water. "I think it's hot. How about I check on the fire?"

"Sounds good. I'll finish this, then bring the chocolate and stuff."

I had a maid, but I actually enjoyed doing stuff for myself. Except windows. No one liked doing windows. I finished cleaning the dishes, then grabbed the s'more stuff and walked into the living room. Achilles was stoking the fire. His bag was propped against the sofa and I eyed it. It was one of those military rucksacks. He turned to me and I handed him the goods. I sat on the floor right in front of the fireplace and Achilles stretched out on his side next to me. We sat there and watched the flames licking up.

"Why did you want to join the military?" Achilles asked softly. "Weren't you into music?"

"Yeah, but joining would have taken me away from home." I punctured a marshmallow with one of the sticks I kept by the fireplace and held it near the flames, browning it. "Between Holden and Jinx, I stayed put."

Achilles grabbed a stick and placed his own marshmallow near the fire. He seemed to be concentrating hard, like he wanted to ask me something, but didn't know how.

"What is it?" I asked.

"I can't see you as a soldier. Not that you're not physically fit to be one, but your attitude would have gotten you smoked."

"Oh, you mean my utter lack of caring?" I snickered.

"If you hold a combat boot to your ear, do you know what you'll hear?"

"The ocean?" I smiled.

"No, you can hear your first drill sergeant calling you a moron."

"That's good," I laughed. "Cute. Didn't know you had it in you, big guy."

"I do, on occasion, try to have a good time."

"Why is it that you guys hardly ever talk then?"

"It's called keeping it professional. The more time you spend with your charge, the more the lines seem to disappear. In order for us to keep you safe, we can't make it personal."

"But you're here."

"That's different."

"Why is that different?" I narrowed my eyes.

"I am assigned to you, Harley. I'm not the kind of guy who stands in the corner and says nothing. Especially if we're in each other's space all the time."

"Assigned to me? Meaning what?" I wasn't sure if I wanted to know the answer to that question. Was Achilles with me all the damn time because the guys thought I'd do something stupid? Okay, I did a lot of stupid shit, but I'd never tried to off myself.

"I'm keeping you safe."

"From what?"

"Yourself."

"I'm not going to try and kill myself, ya know." I placed my browned marshmallow on the chocolate and grabbed some crackers. I bit into it and moaned.

"I know you wouldn't do it intentionally, but you do get yourself into some pretty precarious situations."

"I'm thrill-seeking, remember?" I grinned and Achilles smiled — just a tad. He reached over and thumbed something off the corner of my mouth.

"Chocolate." He showed me his thumb as proof. "What's on the agenda tomorrow?"

"Studio time. A couple more tracks need to be tweaked." I yawned. I hadn't realized how tired I was until just then. "I think I'm going to hit the sheets. I'm fucking wasted. Want to crash on the couch or do you want the guest room?"

"Couch."

"Okay, I'll get you a blanket." I stood up and glanced over my shoulder as I headed to the linen closet. Achilles was licking his thumb. I didn't know why, but my dick popped up immediately from just watching him. I grabbed a fluffy blanket from the top shelf and went back to the living room. Achilles was just making his own s'more.

"Here ya go. Anything else?"

"No, goodnight, Harley."

"Night."

Chapter 2
Achilles

I watched Harley's ass as he walked back to his room. Part of me wanted to join him, the part that had lost all perspective when it came to Harley Payne. I cursed myself for the thousandth time. I needed to stay focused when it came to Harley. He'd had enough shit in his life without adding me to the mix. I needed to keep him safe, and that was all. He didn't remember kissing me back in L.A., and I wasn't going to bring it up. I thought for sure he'd say something the next morning, but he didn't remember any of it.

Not the pool.

Nothing.

I talked a lot with Jinx and the other guys, so I knew Harley hadn't had it easy. Especially when it came to his parents. I was an only child, so I didn't know what it was like to have a sibling.

I leaned back on my elbows and watched the fire. I'd done my homework and I didn't like what I saw. Harley's older brother was killed in combat and although Harley *seemed* fine on the outside, he was anything but. I was lucky enough to be raised and loved by my parents. I was born in New York, but my parents moved back to Greece when I was ten. My grandparents had died in a car crash and left their restaurant to my parents. My father had his own company in Greece and my mother ran the restaurant. Sometimes I'd go just to help out in the kitchen. The place was still very successful, even now. I held dual citizenship, so I went back and forth between the U.S. and Greece a lot.

I moved back to the U.S. and joined the military at eighteen. On a range day six months later, I impressed one of the visiting colonels. I was sent straight to sniper school and became part of Delta Force not long after. I was one of the youngest who had ever been hand-picked for Delta.

The skills I learned in training suit my bodyguard job perfectly. Being stealthy while guarding someone like Harley was a must some days. Harley was always surprised when I popped up right next to him, but if he knew me even a little bit, he'd know I could stand in a room with him and he'd never even know I was there.

I tilted my head to the side and heard Harley getting in the shower. My dick hardened at the thought of his body slicked with soap—what I could do to that body. I squeezed my eyes shut and took a deep breath. I'd always been gay, I knew it at the age of thirteen when I was checking out the local boys on the beach. My parents didn't even bat an eyelash when I told them. Once I joined the military, a whole new world opened up to me and I found out that a lot of guys were gay. They just kept it quiet. My first boyfriend was actually my spotter. We spent countless hours together and ended up kissing one night. Brian and I were together for two years before the night that he was taken from me.

I balled my fist and squeezed my eyes shut. I'd lost him that day in Ramadi when all hell had broken loose. I took a deep, calming breath and opened my eyes, staring into the orange and blue flames of the fire. Three years later and I could still smell the gunpowder in the air, the sounds of screaming, and the fierce burn of multiple bullets entering me. I tried so hard to protect the guys around me, still firing off rounds with most of my right arm hanging by a thread. Then the Apache helicopter swooped in and decimated everything in sight.

I had woken up in a hospital in Germany four months later with my parents at my side. When my time was up, I got out. Then I met Mac Collins; he was the owner of Collins Security. A former Master Sergeant in the Navy, Mac hired guys such as me to run his business. Between bodyguards and assassins, Mac had a go-to business, it seemed.

I came on as a bodyguard, mostly because I'd seen enough death in my time. I saw a shrink to help me deal with my time in the military and what had happened to me. I still had nights when I woke up a sweaty mess, but they were few and far between at this point. I could understand Paul Vincent, the band's old manager and former guitarist, a little better now. He'd gone through a car crash with Gareth Wolf and Ransom Fox, and the result was a damaged hand, PTSD and clinical depression. Paul grew up with the guys and they formed Skull Blasters together. When Gareth came out, Paul took that opportunity to send Gareth threatening letters and tried to scare him out of the band.

I still remember flying across the room when Paul had pulled a gun on Gareth. I had been too late, though, and the gun went off, shooting Axel Blaze. Paul was currently in a mental hospital getting help. I smiled thinking about Axel. His babysitting job turned into something more, and he and Gareth were now married.

The water shut off in the other room and I closed my eyes. I could almost see Harley climbing into bed. I hadn't been with anyone for a long time, and now I was starting to feel something for Harley. I didn't know what it was about him. He could be infuriating, reckless and irresponsible, but he was also very loving and caring with the rest of the band. Then there was the way he looked. He was shorter than me by a few inches, but he was quite built. His smile was what drew me to him immediately, that and his eyes.

Harley was so full of life, it pained me to know he wasn't truly living it. He was stuck in the past and tried to extract love from two people who should have been giving it freely. I knew what it was like to be fractured, to have shards of yourself lying this way and that, and it took a strong person to glue himself back together. I knew Harley could do it. He just had to want it bad enough.

I leaned back against the couch and sighed. Tomorrow would be another day. Another day of watching Harley fly apart on the inside, pieces of him slowly dropping off until there was no more.

I wasn't going to let that happen.

~*~

My eyes sprang open and I checked my watch. I'd slept for four hours, which was plenty for me. It was still dark outside as I crept into the kitchen and started making coffee. I checked on Harley and found him asleep on his back, one hand behind his head. He looked so peaceful just then, like everything that was raging inside him was quiet for the moment. Just watching him, I knew that I was there for a reason. That it was no accident I was chosen to watch over Harley. I'd always believed in fate and destiny, and Harley was mine.

I put together a breakfast of bacon, eggs and some biscuits, and then I cleaned up as quietly as I could in the bathroom. Harley needed his rest; it was evident to me, even if it wasn't to him. Three hours later, a sleepy Harley wandered into the kitchen where I was sitting with my coffee and reading the paper.

"What's all this?" Harley lifted the lid on one of the pans and sniffed.

"You need to eat more." I eyed him over the top of the paper.

Harley made himself a plate and grabbed a cup of coffee, then sat down with me at the table. He ate a bite and looked over at me in surprise.

"This is really good. What did you add?"

"Secret recipe." I lifted a brow. "My mom taught me how to cook. She said whoever I ended up with would appreciate it."

"Um," Harley sipped his coffee. "Were you ever married?"

"No. Haven't found the right one yet." Although, I had a sneaky suspicion *the one* was sitting right across from me.

"Dated?"

I set the newspaper down and pinned Harley with a look. "What do you really want to know?"

"Nothing. Sorry I asked," Harley muttered.

"What about you?" I threw it back at him. "Serious with anyone?"

Harley snorted. "Nope. I don't have time for a relationship."

That was a crock of shit. Harley had time, especially in between tours. It was his parents who kept him from being with anyone. The guy didn't think he deserved to be loved.

"Are you running with me this morning as well?" Harley asked.

"If you'd like."

"I'd like to see if you can beat me," Harley smirked.

"You do realize I was in the military, right?" I reminded him.

"Yes. But you've been out for how long?"

"You're never really out, Harley."

~*~

We took off after eating and Harley was ahead of me. His house sat up against a mountain, and trees surrounded it. I kept a good pace behind him, keeping my breathing steady, and watched the landscape as I did. We were about an hour in when Harley came to a stop. He leaned up against a tree and wiped his forehead. I stood next to him, offering him my bottle of water.

"Damn," Harley panted. "How are you not breathing hard?"

"I'm used to running with a hundred pounds on my back, Harley. I've scaled buildings, hopped from rooftop to rooftop, all with said one hundred pounds on my back. I can run for miles and never get tired."

"You're a machine." Harley coughed, sipping my water.

"I'm a soldier, Harley. Like I said, you never really stop being one."

"Wanna go for a swim?"

"In your guitar pool?" I snickered. Harley's pool was actually in the shape of guitar.

"Yup."

"Sounds good."

We walked back to Harley's house. I think he'd overdone it trying to beat me. The thought made me smile and Harley cocked a brow at me as we entered his back yard.

"Why are you so chipper?" he asked, removing his shirt.

I glanced around the yard. The weather was cold, but the pool was in its own building off to the side. Slate rock covered Harley's patio, and a table with six chairs was underneath a covered section with tiki torches all around. It had a Hawaiian feel to it. Harley was waiting for me to answer. I shrugged and began removing my own shirt. I walked past him and heard an audible gasp from behind me. I stopped and sighed, hanging my head. I'd totally forgotten about my tattoo.

"Achilles," Harley said slowly. "What is your tattoo?"

"I think you know since you have one of your own." I stood still as Harley's footsteps resounded on the slate floor behind me. He was right at my back and I cursed under my breath.

"You have a Valkyrie on your back," he marveled softly.

"So do you," I pointed out.

"But...why?"

I turned to face him. His mouth was slightly agape, but I couldn't blame him. I'd seen his tattoo. It was almost identical to mine.

"Where did you get yours?" I asked.

"My brother. He wasn't just a jock or a soldier, he was an awesome artist. He drew it a long time ago, just before he entered the military. He said that a lot of the guys believed that when they died on the battlefield, they would go to Valhalla."

"Mine represents almost the same thing, but being who I am and what I've done, mine serves a purpose. It's there to remind me that although there is a dark place inside me that allows me to do the things I need to do, I have to remember that there is also a place inside me to protect. I can't ever lose that or I'll be a monster."

"What do you mean?" Harley tilted his head.

"I was a sniper, Harley. I had to take lives to protect the innocent. A part of me, that dark, ugly part, was equipped to deal with that. I needed a reminder that there is a light inside of me as well, a light that reminds me that I have a soul."

"I've seen you, you know. I would never think you were a monster. You take care of people, Achilles. Why would you ever think you're a monster?"

"Because I have it in me, Harley. I wouldn't have been able to do my job if I didn't. The day we were ambushed, I killed so many people, Harley. My guys were dying all around me and I was..." I turned away from him. "I didn't care, do you understand? I took those lives and I didn't fucking care. I wanted them to pay, to suffer horrendously for what they'd done."

Harley's hand crept into mine and he turned me back to face him. I was expecting disgust or pity, what I saw was anger.

"Don't you ever apologize for what you did, do you understand? My brother," Harley stopped, took a deep breath, and continued. "He didn't die right away. They tortured him first." Harley wiped at his eyes. "So don't ever apologize for what you did."

"I'm so sorry," I whispered.

"Holden knew going in that it could happen one day. I got to talk to him a week before he died. We were online, laughing and talking about how we were going to take the bike out on the highway. I needed it, ya know? My parents were the same as they'd always been, but it was really starting to bother me. Then he died, and it was like, I don't know, like somehow I didn't exist anymore. At least before, they kinda talked to me. They'd ask me to take out the trash or pick up the mail, go grocery shopping. When Holden died, the silence was so loud."

I wiped the tear that cascaded down his cheek with my thumb.

"I don't know why I'm telling you all of this," Harley snuffled.

"Because you've had enough, I think. Or at least, I hope you have. Did you get Holden's letter?"

"What letter?" Harley asked, confused.

"When we deployed, we all wrote letters to loved ones, in case we didn't come back. Every soldier does it; well, almost every soldier."

"Did you?"

"Yes, I did, but my parents never got it because I was in Germany in the hospital. Somehow, I lived."

"I'm glad, Achilles. I know I bitch, whine and moan, but I'm glad you're here."

"How 'bout we swim?" I motioned to the pool. "I think my sweat is freezing to my back."

"It's not that cold," Harley laughed.

"To you," I pointed out.

"Come on."

We spent the next hour in the pool. Harley was laughing, and the sound of it bounced off the walls. It was good to hear him laugh. I wanted to smack myself for having let my guard down. There was a reason I'd kept my distance from Harley. I knew about his tattoo, I'd seen it in California when the guys were there for *Singers*. I didn't want to have to explain it, to see the look on his face when he found out exactly what kind of person I was.

We dried off and stepped back into the heated house. Harley went to take a shower as I checked my emails and messages. Harley came out of his room dressed, still drying his hair. I grabbed my rucksack and flung it over my shoulder.

"Okay, I'll take you to the studio, then I'm going to head home and clean up. I'll come back with the Tomahawk and meet you there."

"You have a home?" Harley snickered.

"Yes, I do. I live with Buster and Hammer. Stan set us up in a house among all of you."

"You don't have to take me, you know. I can drive."

"I figured you'd want to drive the bike back home." I cocked a brow.

"You'd let me...drive it?" Harley gaped at me.

"Of course. Just don't wreck it with me on the back."

Harley grinned and ducked his head, and I swore my heart fluttered in my chest. What the fuck? I needed to man up, dammit.

I dropped Harley off and continued on to the house Stan had rented for me, Buster and Hammer. Both of their vehicles were in the driveway as I pulled in. Unlike me, they didn't have one guy specifically assigned to them. I jumped out of my truck and strode up the walk, unlocking the door. Hammer was in the kitchen making something and Buster sat at the table reading the paper.

"Marc, Kirk." I nodded as I walked in.

"How's Harley?" Hammer asked.

I sat down at the kitchen table and Marc, otherwise known as Hammer, brought me coffee. I'd sparred with him. 'Hammer' fits him nicely.

"We had an emotional moment yesterday, but I'm convinced what he and his parents are going through is repressed grief."

"That guy is going to explode," Buster said quietly, shaking his head.

"I have to get him away from his parents. He needs to heal, and he can't do that when he's with them. He deserves to be happy, goddammit."

Hammer sat down and eyed me closely. "Did we cross a line?"

"No. I haven't acted on how I feel." I leaned back in the chair and folded my arms across my chest, glaring at him.

"Maybe you should," Buster suggested.

"What? You know I can't do that!"

"I don't know, Kirk has a point," Hammer added. "Maybe if Harley knew that someone cared for him, it would make things easier somehow."

"He has friends who care for him," I pointed out.

"Look, how long do you think you can keep your feelings for him a secret? Kirk and I figured it out after a week."

"He's not ready." I shook my head vehemently.

"He isn't, or you aren't?" Hammer cocked a brow.

"I'm going to get showered. I'm meeting Harley over at the studio. What are you guys up to today?"

"Making sure the other ones don't get into trouble," Hammer chuckled.

My phone shrilled and I looked down at the caller I.D. Mac Collins was calling.

"I think our plans just changed."

Chapter 3
Achilles

I chuckled softly into my headset as Mac paced before a group of recruits. They were all fitted with vests for this training exercise. I held the rifle that would set those vests off. Hammer and Buster were in the trees about a half-mile from me. I was in a ghillie suit covered in pine needles and cones.

"Spread out, boys, and don't get dead," Mac shouted.

I had the perfect vantage spot to watch the newest recruits. Maybe half of them would make it. The first shout floated across the forest and I cracked a grin. One of the recruits crested my hill and I shot him, his vest filling the air with beeping noises.

"Fuck!" he yelled.

One by one, they were all picked off by either me, Buster or Hammer. The last recruit was trying to belly-crawl back to the safe point, his eyes taking in his surroundings warily. When the other recruits walked out into the open, he stood up and began yelling.

"Hell, yeah! I made it!"

I jumped to my feet right behind him and put my blade to his throat.

"Now you're dead," I whispered in his ear.

"Holy fuck. Where the hell did you come from?" he asked.

"Guys, meet Achilles." Mac gestured to me. "Our resident sniper."

I removed my knife from the guy's throat and strode across the forest in my suit. Most of the recruits were staring at me wide-eyed as I reached Mac's side.

"I know you!" One of them pointed at me. "Your picture is on the wall at sniper school!"

"Yes, it is," Mac acknowledged. "And none of you will ever replace it. Seems you've been out of the military for too long, boys. We're going to have to pound it back into you. Hammer, Buster! Take the boys for a run, will ya?"

I chuckled as they all groaned and fell in line with Hammer and Buster. I removed my jacket, sipping from one of the water bottles Mac provided. Mac leaned against the bed of his truck, eyeing me.

"You sure you don't want to transfer to wet work, Achilles? We could use a guy like you."

"I'm done with death, Mac, but thanks."

"Yeah, I get that. How's everything else? Harley not wearing you out too much, is he?"

I choked on my water and Mac grinned.

"Harley is...well, he's better."

"If you've got some down time, I'd like you to work with a few of these guys. They have potential."

"I can't say when I'd have down time, but I'll definitely look into it. Some of these guys are too cocky."

"And Axel will beat it right out of them during combatives," Mac snickered.

"So will Hammer." I laughed.

~*~

I drove out to the studio after I'd showered and dressed. I took the side entrance, hoping to not cause a disturbance. Harley was sitting on a stool in the corner with a guitar, and I stepped behind the wall, just watching him. He strummed the strings lightly and then began singing. I knew the song, "More Than Words" by Extreme.

His eyes were closed and I marveled at how gorgeous he looked sitting there. How could anyone treat him like he didn't make a difference? Like he didn't matter? I stepped back further when Gareth entered the room. He sat down on the adjacent stool and picked up his own guitar, joining Harley in the song.

I was rooted to the spot. They sounded fabulous together. The first time I'd heard Harley sing was at Halloween. He had a voice that was smooth as silk and a presence on stage that commanded attention. His hair hung in his eyes as he played, the lyrics flowing from him easily. I crept forward a bit as Ransom and Rebel joined them. It was easy to understand how they had come this far. Their love for one another, the friendship and respect they each had was evident. It wasn't just one member of the band who shone. It was all of them.

They wrapped up the song and Ransom slapped Harley on the back playfully.

"One of these days, people are going to realize I'm not the lead singer," he joked.

"I'm happy where I am, Ransom." Harley took Ransom's hand.

I cleared my throat and stepped into the room. Gareth grinned and waved.

"Hey, Achilles."

"Gareth." I nodded and leaned against the wall. "Guys."

"Okay, let's work on 'Monkey Sex'," Ransom announced.

I spluttered and Ransom chuckled. "Yes, it is a song," he affirmed.

"Jinx?" I chuckled.

"Yup." Gareth laughed. "It's a good song, really."

I watched as the guys got their equipment together. Jinx had already banged out his part of the track, I guessed. The guys worked around it, the lyrics made me snort.

You're in my head, get in my bed
I'm in your head, get in my bed.
Want you screaming and writhing under me
We'd make perfect monkey sex, can't you see?

Harley and Gareth stood together, both of them trying not to laugh as they sang. For two hours, I was treated to the guys working their magic. Once they agreed that they were done for the day, Harley set his guitar down and the guys all looked over the other tracks.

"Jinx should be back next week or so." Ransom pointed to the paper. "We should start with 'Fire it Up' when he returns."

"I agree." Harley tilted his head. "We need to finish tracks thirteen and fourteen. The rest of them should go quickly once we're all here."

"I really want to take my time with this one. I'm not sure I'm ready to tour yet. Besides, I wouldn't want us to go on tour right when London Boys is ending theirs. Jinx and Jayden need to spend some quality time together." Ransom ran a hand through his hair.

"I would like to spend some time with my husband," Gareth agreed.

"Where is Axel?" Ransom asked.

"Training new recruits." Gareth beamed.

"Oh hell," I muttered. They all turned to look at me and I pasted a fake smile on. "They'll have so much fun."

"Yeah, right," Gareth chuckled. "I've sat in on one of his training sessions."

"Damn! It's five already?" Ransom exhaled loudly. "Where did the day go?"

"Dinner?" Harley asked.

"I could use some food." Gareth nodded.

"All right, let's head out." Harley gingerly set his guitar down and eyed me with a grin. "Did ya bring it?"

"Yes. Don't go crazy," I answered.

"Bring what?" Rebel tilted his head.

"Come outside." I motioned to them.

We stepped out of the studio and Rebel let out a gasp. My silver Tomahawk was resting off to the side of their vehicles. Rebel walked over to it, letting out an impressed whistle as he ran his hands across the shiny chrome.

"Damn, Achilles!" Rebel enthused. "This is fucking *hot*! How the fuck did you get it?"

"I know people," I answered vaguely.

"You can't even use these on public roads! How the fuck did you manage it?" Rebel kept on.

"I don't give a shit?" I replied with a grin.

"Are you James Bond?" Ransom squatted in front of the Tomahawk.

"I wish," I chuckled. I glanced over at Harley. "You know some back roads to wherever we're going?"

"Yep." Harley smiled knowingly.

"Well, let's head out to the diner," Ransom laughed.

"Sounds good," Harley replied gleefully.

Harley ran his hand down the side of my bike and I actually shivered. I knew my bike was impressive. Only a handful had been made and they weren't even considered motorcycles because of the four wheels. Harley straddled the bike and I climbed on back. I wrapped my arms around his middle and Harley stiffened. I leaned in a bit and spoke in his ear.

"What's wrong?"

"Nothing," he answered quickly. "You might want to hold on tighter."

"Don't kill me," I joked.

Harley fired up the Tomahawk and I handed him a helmet, putting on my own. I gripped him tightly as he lurched out of the driveway and took a side street behind the buildings. I always had a sense of being free on my bike, as if the whole world didn't exist and I was in my own make believe world. Flying free with Harley was a different feeling altogether. His body moved fluidly with the Tomahawk, as if it were actually meant for him. He came to a stop behind the diner and I climbed off, setting my helmet in the saddlebag. Harley got off and took his helmet off. A huge grin was plastered on his face as he handed me the helmet.

"What a fucking ride!"

"Glad you liked it."

"Tell me I can do that again sometime?"

If it kept that smile on his face, I'd let him ride it every damn day. I nodded and Harley clapped his hands together. I laughed and followed him inside the diner. The guys had grabbed a table, and I sat off to the side, trying to stay inconspicuous. I watched him as he sat and joked with the guys. This was the Harley I wanted to see, not the one who looked like his life was over every time he visited his parents. I balled my fists under the table as I thought about Harley's life.

"Achilles?"

"Yes?" I answered automatically. I glanced over to see Harley eyeing me with a worried look.

"You look…mad. Is everything okay?"

"I'm fine, I promise," I assured him.

I was battling my attraction to the guy every day and I was fine?

Ha.

I ate, but I didn't taste it. I was too preoccupied with watching Harley as he laughed with the guys. There were times I could see that happiness right under the surface, but when Harley went home, the sadness was back. I wanted to heal him, to tell him he was so much more than he knew. I was still trying to reach the surface, kicking and screaming to break it; what good was I to Harley if I wasn't whole either? Part of me was still lying in that desert, listening to my fellow soldiers dying in the night. I'd seen a shrink, but they could only do so much.

Harley stole one of the French fries off my plate and dunked it in ketchup. He turned to me with a grin and I cracked a smile. He was so childlike at times, I forget he's older than me.

"You didn't want that, right?" Harley waggled the fry in front of me.

"No. I'm done. Have at it."

Harley searched my features closely and then leaned in, lowering his voice. "Are you sure you're okay?"

"You don't have to worry about me, Harley. I'm here for you, not the other way around."

"Tough shit. I'm not blind, and I can see that something is wrong."

I glanced around the crowded table and shook my head. I wasn't going to vomit my woes onto these guys.

"You're coming to my house after this," he ordered.

"I kind of have to, remember?"

"You're not just going to drop me off is what I mean."

"How do you know something is wrong with me? Maybe I'm just quiet." I glared at him, hoping he'd back off.

"I've spent months with you, Achilles. Were you quiet? Yes. Are you still? No. I think I know you just enough to see when something is bothering you. I'd like to think we're friends."

Friends? Oh God, I wanted so much more from Harley than friendship, but that wasn't my call, and I was going to be the good bodyguard and leave my charge alone. At least, sexually. I couldn't deny the fact that I'd wanted him from the second I'd laid eyes on him; Harley wasn't just good looking, he was kind-hearted and funny. He had "California surfer" written all over him, from his light brown hair with highlights, to his caramel-brown eyes — not to mention his copper-tanned skin and rocking body.

"Achilles?"

"Yes?"

"Where did you go? I'm worried about you now. You look like you're trying to take a shit."

I laughed at that and the whole table stopped talking and looked right at me. I shrugged, grunted a little, and they went back to their conversations.

"I'm just in my own little world right now," I tried to explain.

Harley leaned in and placed his hand on my arm. I looked down at where his hand was, then back to his eyes. Our eyes met and I swore I saw something in Harley's. Not sure what, but it was there. Maybe I was seeing what I wanted to see, a mutual attraction, even though Harley was as straight as they came — or I thought he was. The kiss in the bathroom in L.A. wasn't that of a straight man.

"Why don't we head out?" he asked softly.

"Did you eat enough?" I asked.

"I ate all your fries." Harley gave me a sheepish grin.

I looked down at my plate. Sure enough, Harley had eaten all my fries.

"Okay. Let's go."

After saying bye to the guys, Harley straddled my bike once more, but he let me drive. I looked over my shoulder at him as he snapped his helmet on.

"Don't feel like taking her for a spin?" I asked.

"Maybe some other time. I'm not feeling so hot all of a sudden."

"What did you drink?" I turned partially on the bike and touched his cheek. He felt a little warm.

"Just soda."

"Maybe you're coming down with something?"

"Maybe." Harley nodded and tipped his head back, inhaling the cool air.

"Let's get you home."

I pulled out of the parking lot and stopped. Something felt off and I couldn't put my finger on it.

"What is it?" Harley asked.

"It's nothing, I guess." I placed his hand on my abdomen. "Hang on, okay?"

Harley wrapped his arms around my waist and I pulled out into the alley behind the diner. I retraced Harley's path and made it back to his place in ten minutes. I pulled into his driveway and helped him off the bike. Harley wobbled a bit, so I held on to him. I removed his helmet and checked him thoroughly.

"You're a little warm. I don't like it." I peered into his eyes. They were glazed over. "Maybe you should see a doctor."

"Nah, I'm good. I'll get over whatever this is. I don't get sick often."

"Which is why I'd like you to see a doctor, Harley." Harley slumped in my arms and exhaled loudly. I held him up and his head fell back, a lazy smile turned his lips.

"S'all good, Achiiillleees," Harley slurred.

"Okay, that's it." I picked Harley up and carried him into the house. I set him down on his bed and took off his shoes. Harley rolled to his side with a sigh and curled into the fetal position. I covered him with a comforter and headed into the kitchen to use the phone. The phone number for the band's personal doctor was on the fridge and I called him immediately.

"Doc Mathis here," he answered.

"Um, this is Achilles Castellanos, Harley's bodyguard? Um, I think he's sick."

"Well, hello, Achilles. Is he running a fever?"

"He seems warm."

"I'll be there in ten."

I hung up and paced the room. Harley seemed fine at the diner and now he wasn't. Maybe it was food poisoning? I went back to Harley's room to see him leaning over the side of the bed. I ran and grabbed the trashcan just in time to catch Harley puking out dinner.

"Achilles," Harley rasped.

"I'm here." I sat on the edge of the bed and smoothed his hair back.

"Stomach hurts."

"Lay back," I instructed him.

Harley did as he was told, and I rubbed his stomach in soft, slow circles. It was something my mother had done for me whenever I was sick and it helped me. I hoped it helped Harley. Harley sighed and his eyelashes fluttered. Even sick, he was the most gorgeous man I'd ever laid eyes on.

"How's that feel?" I asked.

"Better. You don't look so hot either." Harley motioned to my face.

I blinked and tried to focus on Harley. My stomach lurched and my head began to pound.

"Oh shit," I whispered. I pulled out my phone and dialed Axel's number. He picked up on the second ring.

"Achilles?"

"Sick...Harley's... come."

"Ohhh fuck." My head swam and the gurgling in my gut would not stop. Something cool hit my forehead and then a warm hand touched my temple.

"Harley? It's Doc Mathis. Can you tell me where it hurts?"

"Hurts everywhere. Feel like my stomach's ripping apart."

"Seems like you and Achilles have the same thing. What did you eat or drink today?"

"Achilles is sick?" I tried to sit up, but Doc Mathis pushed me back down gently.

"He's in the living room. He's already thrown up everything he possibly can and I'm giving him anti-nausea medication. It's the same thing I'm going to give you. Both of you are hooked up to IVs, so please be careful. I'm going to prescribe you bed rest and don't remove your IV until all the saline is gone from the bag, okay? If you or Achilles feels any worse, I want you to call me immediately."

"What's wrong with us, Doc?"

"I suspect food poisoning. I'm giving you forty-eight hours, and if you don't improve, I'll be drawing blood and admitting you."

"Are you sure Achilles is okay?" I asked, holding my head.

"Yes, he's got a huge guy in there with him," Doc assured me. "Get some sleep, Harley."

As much as I tried to fight it, whatever the doc had given me knocked me the fuck out.

I woke up and felt a presence next to me. I turned my head to see Gareth fast asleep next to me. His long, black lashes touched his skin and his breathing was soft and even. I sat up a bit and realized Gareth and I weren't alone. Axel was sitting in the corner chair with a cup of coffee and a magazine. He looked up when he noticed I was awake, and smiled.

"Well, how was your 12 hour nap?" he asked.

"Wait. What? I've been asleep that long? Where's Achilles? Is he okay?"

"Whoa, one thing at a time. Calm down, Achilles is fine. I just looked in on him. He's still asleep."

"What the hell happened?" I rubbed my head.

"Doc seems to think it was food poisoning. I took out your IV a bit ago, so you can take a shower if you're up to it. I've also made food for you and Achilles."

"How long have you and Gareth been here?"

"Since Achilles called me. He got three words out and I was on my way. Gareth insisted on coming and when Doc told him you were sick, he crawled in bed with you and held you while you cried."

"I cried?" I furrowed my brows.

"Oh yeah. Cried, threw up, shit, you name it, you did it."

"Oh God," I whispered.

"I don't suppose you remember Gareth and I washing you up in the tub, huh?"

"No." I closed my eyes and sighed. They flew open and I stared at Axel. "I was naked?"

"Well, we tried to clean the shit off you fully clothed, but it wasn't working out too well."

I scowled and Axel grinned. Gareth snickered next to me and I pushed his shoulder. He sat up and hugged me so tightly, I thought he'd break a rib on me.

"Hey, now. I'm okay," I murmured in his ear.

"I was so worried about you!" Gareth practically screamed in my ear.

"Ow, head still hurts a bit."

"Sorry," Gareth apologized. "You had us worried."

I climbed out of the bed and held onto the nightstand to steady myself. I was still a bit woozy and my eyesight was a tad blurry. Axel moved to my side and wrapped an arm around my waist.

"Where are you going?" he asked.

"I need to see Achilles."

Axel helped me into the living room and there, wrapped in a blanket, was Achilles. His face was pale, but he looked okay. I sat down next to him and ran my fingers through his hair. His eyelashes fluttered and then his gray eyes were fixed on me.

"Hey," he croaked. "How are you feeling?"

"Better. How do you feel?" I asked, palming his cheek.

Achilles took my hand and held it. His eyes searched mine and I lowered mine at the intensity of his gaze.

"I was worried about you," he whispered.

"Um, both of you should shower. I can smell you from here." Gareth pinched his nose.

I had to smile at the slight flush of color on Achilles' cheeks. Neither one of us was going to win any awards for our stench. I got up and headed back to my room on much more stable feet.

"Fine. I'll go shower."

"Then you'll eat," Axel called after me.

Ugh. Food did not sound good right now, and my stomach seconded that with a slight rumble. I stood under the hot spray and just let it wash over me. I washed up, making sure I cleaned my ass crack thoroughly. I felt slightly better as I got out and toweled off. I threw on some clothes and found Gareth waiting for me in my room.

"Hey, Munchkin."

"You scared me." Gareth searched my features.

"I'm okay, I swear. Was anyone else sick?"

"No, just you and Achilles."

"That's odd." My brows scrunched in thought. "Is he in the shower?"

"Yes. Axel had to help him there, and I don't think he wanted you to see him like that anyway."

I sat down on the bed and rubbed my face with my hands. I was seriously worried about Achilles. He didn't look good. I looked a ton better, but Achilles? Not so much. Gareth took my hand and I looked up at him.

"He'll be okay," Gareth assured me. "Now, come eat."

I followed Gareth into my kitchen where food awaited me, courtesy of Axel. I stared at it and sat down, grabbing a biscuit first. Hopefully, the bread would stay down and then I could move onto something else. I sipped my juice and took a bite, waiting for the urge to puke to rise again. Axel came into the kitchen and kissed Gareth's head on his way to the coffee maker. Never in a million years would I have thought I'd see Munchkin married to a former SEAL, but there they were. I grinned as Gareth smiled at his husband adoringly.

"Axel and I went shopping for you while you were asleep," Gareth informed me.

"Why?"

"Because we don't know what made you sick. In my experience, it could be anything, so I threw out all your food and bought new stuff."

"Thank you." I shoved another bite of biscuit in my mouth. Axel sat down next to Gareth and rubbed his back, kissing his temple.

"Okay, thanks so much for coming by, but I can't take the two of you and your googly eyes."

"Are you sure?" Gareth eyed me.

"I feel so much better. Thank you, guys, for coming over and taking care of us. I really do appreciate it," I said sincerely.

"If you need anything, and I mean anything, you call, yeah?" Axel placed his hand on my forehead and nodded. "You're much cooler. Achilles is back on the couch. He showered, and I think that was enough for him. Keep an eye on him, yeah?"

"I will."

I closed the door behind Gareth and Axel, and went to my room. In the back of my closet was where I hid my stress relief. I looked over my shoulder cautiously as I removed my crayons and coloring books from a container in the back. I took them to the kitchen, stopping in the living room to make sure Achilles was still asleep and breathing normally. I sat down and opened the crayon box, checking them to make sure they were still sharp and didn't need to be sharpened.

Holden and I, when we were kids, used to color all the time and I found that it relaxed me when things were stressful. It was a habit I kept to this day. I must have colored hundreds of books when he died, just hoping I'd somehow feel better. I grabbed my favorite one and opened the page to a smiling bear with honey. The stress ebbed away as I started with the crayon inside the lines and colored them in with even strokes.

"What are you doing?"

I almost jumped sky-high at Achilles' voice behind me. I tried to cover up what I was doing, to no avail.

"Are you...coloring?" Achilles bent over me, staring at my coloring book.

"Yeah? What of it? I find it relaxing," I defended.

"Relaxing, eh?" A small, sly smile formed on Achilles' lips.

"Don't judge me!" I pointed at him with my crayon.

"Fine, I won't. Let me try it then."

"No. You'll probably color outside the lines and break my crayons."

Achilles chuckled and sat down across from me. "I promise not to press down too hard, and I'll stay inside the lines."

I narrowed my eyes at him and held my crayons to my chest.

"Come on." Achilles motioned to the coloring books. "Just give me one."

"Fine. You can have Eeyore."

"What if I want Pooh?"

I shot him a look and he grinned.

"Fine, Eeyore it is."

"You look...better." I let my eyes wander over his face.

"I feel better." Achilles removed a blue crayon from the box and began outlining his character.

I watched in fascination as his big hands gently colored inside the lines, the way his fingers glided over the picture effortlessly.

"Harley?"

"Huh?"

"I asked if his bow was pink or red."

"Oh, um, it's pink. I think." I bit my lip in concentration as I worked on my honey pot.

"That's really good." Achilles motioned to my picture. "What other books do you have?"

I pulled my stack off the chair and Achilles thumbed through them. He finished the one he'd started and scribbled his name at the bottom. I smiled and looked up at him.

"I do that, too."

"Well, people should know who created this masterpiece." Achilles lifted the picture and smiled.

"That's really good. I'm surprised."

"Why?"

"Because you're this huge guy, it just seems weird."

"You should get newer ones. I think they have some online."

"I just pick them up at the store. I don't really order stuff online, mostly because I'm not here enough to get it."

"Well, I'm going to get you some new ones."

"Why?"

"Because it is relaxing, and now I want to do it."

I chuckled and Achilles smiled at me. Jesus, he had a great smile. I ducked my head and finished my character, scribbling my name at the bottom.

"What do you think? Is it fridge worthy?" I asked.

"I think it is." Achilles stood and took my paper to the fridge. He placed magnets on the four corners and stepped back, admiring it. "Now this is art."

My smile faded as I recalled my parents taking down my English paper from the fridge. I'd been so proud to get an "A" that I put it up, hoping they'd see it and tell me how proud they were of me. It ended up in Holden's room on his "this stuff is awesome" corkboard. Then, Holden had made me a cake and we celebrated on the floor of his room.

"Hey, are you okay?" Achilles asked.

"Just remembering some stuff."

"Oh?"

"It seems like every good thing I did, Holden was the one who celebrated with me. If I got an 'A' he made a cake. If I got a 'B' he'd make a cupcake." I chuckled at the memory.

"He was an extraordinary man, wasn't he? I wish I could have met him."

"He would have loved you. You guys had a lot in common."

"We do?"

"Holden loved guns and explosives, it was one of the reasons he couldn't wait to join the military. He skipped college and went right in. I thought for sure my parents would have a coronary, but Holden could do no wrong."

"They favored him, didn't they?"

"Yes, they did. Funny thing? I didn't care, I loved him so much and he treated me like I was the best thing that ever happened to him."

"I'm not a big fan of explosives, but I can hold my own with a gun."

"You and Rebel should hang out." I laughed. "He's got tons of guns. His grandfather thinks we'll be at war with ourselves soon."

"Grandfather?" Achilles asked.

"Yeah, Rebel had it rough, but he's managed to jump over some very high hurdles. I'm in awe of him." Achilles' stomach growled and I smiled. "Hungry?"

"I am, which is surprising."

"Axel made food. I put it in the oven for you. He said they went grocery shopping. They threw everything away that was in the house."

"Makes sense." Achilles brows furrowed.

"What is it?"

"No one else got sick, just the two of us. We all ordered almost the same exact thing, so why us? I hardly ever get sick, and food poisoning isn't something I've ever had. My stomach is like iron after the hell I went through in the military."

"Don't know. I just know I never want to feel that way again." I shuddered.

"Well, we can both eat and then maybe hang out and watch some TV?"

"Don't you have someone else you'd rather hang with?"

Achilles leaned forward and gave me a sparkling smile. "Maybe I like hanging out with you."

I glared at him, but he wouldn't budge. That damn smile still in place.

"Fine." I exhaled loudly, hoping Achilles would think I didn't want him there. Truth be told, he chased away the silence and made me feel…wanted. Too bad it was just his job to hang out with me. I knew the guys thought I was a loose cannon, and in a way, I was. I also knew I had disappointed them at times with my behavior.

Achilles and I cleaned up the table and ate some more food. We ended up on the couch, lounging and watching stupid TV shows.

"See? If that was me out there, that fucker would be thrown off the island immediately," Achilles practically snorted.

"Why? That's the whole point of the show. It's reality TV, fuck each other over and all that. Form alliances and then stab people in the back to win."

"They wouldn't last five seconds in the desert."

I sat up on my elbow and eyed him. "Were you scared?"

"I let it in, and then I let it go. You have to. A certain degree of terrified is good, you can't go off all half-cocked. You'll get your guys killed."

"Is that what happened to you?" I asked quietly.

"The guy in charge had just come out of officers school. He hadn't spent one second in a real world situation. You can't go by the damn manual in that kind of clusterfuck, so yeah, he got them dead."

"Did he die?"

"He did. I was the only one to make it out alive, and I did it kicking and screaming."

I glanced over at Achilles' biceps. He had some pretty colorful tattoos and Greek letters. I could see just beyond them, though, and the scars were visible.

"Can't hide it all." Achilles ran a hand over his bicep. "I have more scars. I've kept them uncovered to remind me."

"Remind you of what? That day?"

"No, to remind me that I'm still here. They tried and they failed to kill me."

I reached over and took his hand. "I'm glad you're still here."

Something passed between us in that second and I knew I saw something in Achilles' eyes just then. My phone shrilled and we pulled apart like we were on fire. I grabbed it off the coffee table and saw that Jinx was calling. I grinned and swiped "talk."

"Hey!" I said, excitedly.

"I just heard from Gareth that you and Achilles are sick! Are you guys okay? Do I need to come back—"

"I'm okay, I swear it. Achilles is looking much better, too."

Jinx let out an audible breath on the other end and I had to smile. Jinx was one of those guys who would give you the shirt off his back if you needed it. Yeah, he was a former man-whore, but he was one of the best friends I have ever had. I really missed him a lot.

"So how's the tour going for Jayden? He getting used to it yet?"

"He's eating better, I'm making sure of it. He's still tired, but we know how that goes. I'm actually looking forward to going home with him."

"I can't wait to see you. I miss you, man."

"I miss you, too. How's Achilles holding up? You run him into the ground yet?" Jinx chuckled.

"He's just fine." There was a commotion on the other end of the line and then girls screaming. "I'll let you go, sounds like you have your hands full."

"If you need me, just holler. Love ya, man."

"Love you, too." I hung up with a sigh and reclined on the sofa.

"You look beat," Achilles observed.

"I am. Fuck, I'm so tired."

"Go to bed. I'll lock up."

"Are you… staying?" I tried to keep the hope out of my voice.

"Yeah. I'm staying."

I went to bed, but I left my door open. I didn't know why part of me was hoping Achilles would join me. There was just something about him that got to me where no one else ever has. I'd found men attractive in the past, but Achilles was one of those men who stopped you in your tracks and stole your breath. Add in the fact that he was sweet as hell? He was a catch and then some. I chuckled to myself because this was the first time in my life I wanted a man — a straight man, no less. Oh, the irony.

Would I let him fuck me? My dick sat up at that thought and I gripped it, stroking slowly. Achilles bending me over and stuffing his fat cock in my ass. Oh yeah, I'd let him fuck me for sure. I'd seen the outline of his dick when we went swimming. He was not tiny.

I came quietly, trying not to make too much noise as my orgasm overtook me with thoughts of Achilles fucking me swirling in my head. I cleaned up and rolled to my side. I wondered if Achilles ever thought of me in that way. I shook my head and laughed. Pfft, yeah right.

Chapter 5

Harley

A ringing phone woke me at noon. I grabbed it off the nightstand and swiped "talk."

"Yo."

"I heard you were knocking on death's door." Rebel laughed into my ear.

"I'm good now. I feel tons better."

"How's Achilles?"

"I don't know, let me check." I crept out of bed and into the living room. The couch was made and the blankets folded neatly. I searched the whole house before going back to the living room and collapsing on the couch. "Well, he must be better because he's gone."

"He's never *really* gone though, is he? You want to hang tonight? Maybe hit the Green Room?"

"Sounds good. Any locals playing there tonight?"

"Aren't there always? See you at seven?"

"Sounds good. Later."

I hung up and jumped in the shower, moaning at the feel of the water hitting my skin. It felt good and my muscles were sore from puking. I got cleaned up and then got out. My face needed to see a razor, badly. I sprayed some shaving cream into my hand and lathered my face. I was just swiping up my right cheek when movement caught my eye. I froze mid-swipe and cocked my head to the side.

"Harley?" Achilles called from the bedroom.

"In here."

Achilles cracked the door and peered in. "Hey, just came back from my run."

"I thought you'd left," I admitted.

"Not yet. I do need to go home and get changed. Check in with Axel and all that."

"Well, I'm headed to the bar tonight to see Rebel. Do you want to join us?"

"I could maybe swing that. What time?"

"Seven. You don't have to —"

"Oh, I know. I want to." Achilles grinned at me and my stomach fluttered and flip-flopped. Well, now what? I was acting like a chick in love around this guy. I needed to reel this shit in.

"You okay?" Achilles asked.

"Wonderful."

~*~

I got to the bar at six thirty and jumped on one of the stools. Tyler, the bartender, came by and I ordered a Recycling Bin. What the hell, I'd have one and be done with it for the night. A local band was rocking it out on the stage in the back and music thumped over the floorboards. A few of the guys came by now and then and chatted me up before heading off to the back to play their set. I got up and headed for the bathroom. My stomach was doing much better, but I still felt a little off. When I came back out, a woman was sitting at the bar. Her long hair reached the middle of her back and she was wearing six-inch heels and a miniskirt. I sat down and she turned to me with a smile. The face I knew, the boobs I definitely knew.

"Arielle?" I said in astonishment. "What are you doing here?"

"Visiting. Why?"

"Well, the last time I saw you was in California."

"Yes, and you didn't even spend any time with me," Arielle pouted.

"Sorry about that. You know, the show and all. I had to mingle. What were you doing there?"

"Oh, I was auditioning for a movie that Sal Falco was in. He invited me to the party afterward."

"I didn't know you were an actress."

"Aspiring." Arielle flipped her hair back, shoving her boobs out.

"Did you get the part?"

"No. I even tried sleeping with the guy, but no dice." Arielle clucked her tongue. "He's probably gay anyway."

I bit my lip to keep from laughing. Most of us agreed that Sal Falco was probably gay, except for Ransom. We all knew he had the hots for the guy, he owned every movie that Sal Falco had ever made.

"So anyway," I turned on the stool to face her and picked up my pitcher. "Who are you visiting?"

"Hey, Harley."

I glanced over my shoulder to see Rebel behind me, removing his Harley Davidson jacket. His eyes fell on Arielle and he cocked a brow at me.

"You remember Arielle, Rebel?" I motioned to her with my free hand.

"Sure do." Rebel stuck his hand out. "How are you?"

Arielle flipped her hair again and slid off her stool, completely ignoring Rebel. I shot him a what-the-fuck look and he shook his head and smiled.

"Well, nice seeing you." Arielle pulled a jacket over her shoulders and click-clacked her way out of the bar.

"Wow, she didn't even shake my hand and I showered and everything." Rebel cracked up, jumping on the vacated stool.

"To be fair, you look like one of Satan's rejects."

"Excuse me? I'll have you know, I'd be his right hand man." Rebel wiggled his brows.

"That's a load of shit. You went to church every Sunday with your grandmother before she passed, and I know your grandfather keeps a Bible by his bed."

"Shh! People will find out I'm ordinary."

"You are far from it, my friend." I slapped Rebel's shoulder.

"How are you doing? Feeling better and all?"

"Pretty much. I felt like I was dying," I admitted. "I think Achilles got it worse than me because he was still a little pale in the afternoon."

"It's hard to imagine that big guy sick at all," Rebel mused.

From my seat at the bar, I noticed every female head looking at the entrance. I followed their line of sight and sucked in a breath of my own. Achilles was wearing a flannel gray shirt with faded blue jeans and black hiking boots. A matching gray scarf was wrapped around his neck and he wore a black leather jacket. Rebel let out a whistle as Achilles crossed the bar to us.

"Damn, he should have been a model," Rebel said quietly.

"Hey," I greeted. My voice cracked and I tried again. "Hey," I said more firmly.

"You look better." Achilles motioned to my drink. "Are you done with that?"

I looked at my drink and nodded. "I've had a few sips here and there, but I don't want to push it."

"You look good, Achilles," Rebel said with a sly grin.

"I feel better. Much better. At least my stomach doesn't feel like it's liquefying."

We sat around for an hour shooting the shit. Rebel and I discussed the tracks we needed to finish and Achilles listened, but only asked a few questions. He drank water and I couldn't blame him. My stomach felt funky again and I excused myself to go to the bathroom. I washed my hands and looked in the mirror. A line of sweat began to bead at my forehead and my hands shook.

"What the fuck?"

I rinsed my face with cool water and headed back to the bar. Rebel and Achilles were in deep conversation as I walked up. They both clammed up as I sat down.

"What were you two talking about?" I asked, suspicious.

"It's nothing." Rebel shook his head.

"Bullshit." I glared at them both. "Don't treat me like an idiot."

"Fine," Achilles sighed. "I was asking Rebel about your brother."

"What about him?"

"I just wanted to know if Rebel thought he was the kind of guy who would have left a letter. Especially to you, Harley. We both agree that he would."

"I would have gotten it," I argued.

"Would you?" Rebel took my hand.

"They wouldn't." I shook my head. "They wouldn't keep something like that from me."

"Harley." Rebel took my hands.

"No! They wouldn't do that to me!" I shouted.

I pushed away from the bar and ran out the front door. I didn't check to see if Achilles was behind me. I jumped into my truck and floored it out of the parking lot. My head swam and my stomach rumbled as I headed down the back streets. Rain began to fall as I headed towards my parents' house. They wouldn't have kept that from me, would they? I mean, I knew they hated me, but to keep something like that a secret? I screeched to a stop in front of the house and jumped out of the truck. One of the living room lights was on as I trudged up the front walk. I unlocked the door and stepped into the foyer. The TV was on low in the living room and I headed that way. My father was passed out in his chair, a glass of bourbon on the table.

"Wake up!" I shouted, gripping him by the front of his robe. "Where is it?"

"Huh? What? What the hell?" my father slurred.

"Where is it, Dad? Where's the letter Holden wrote to me?"

"What the hell you talkin' bout, boy? What letter?"

I narrowed my eyes. Underneath that bravado, my father was scared shitless.

"You're lying! I know he would have written me a letter! He would have never left me without saying something!"

"What the hell is wrong with you? We didn't get any letter!"

"You didn't, huh? Fine. Watch this shit, *Dad*."

I stomped out of the living room and headed for the garage. I knew where they kept the keys to Holden's bike.

"Where you goin'?!" my father shouted.

"To take what's mine!"

Chapter 6

Achilles

I was out of the bar so fast, I think Rebel's head spun. Harley had a minute on me at the most. I took off down the alley and jumped on my bike. I had a feeling I knew where Harley was going. Rain began to fall as I headed in the direction of the Payne's house. The roads were becoming slick as I rounded the curve to Harley's parents' house. A light lit up the road and I realized it was the garage door opening. Harley shot out on a motorcycle and flew into the street. The back end skidded a bit and then Harley righted it. I knew I could catch him on my Tomahawk, but I didn't want to freak him out.

I followed less than a mile behind him and kept my eyes on the road ahead of me. Harley took the Seventeen exit and I cursed. The roads were getting worse as the rain turned into snow. Harley was going almost ninety as we hit a curve in the road and he seemed to speed up before the next curve ahead of us.

"Slow down, Harley!" I shouted. Not that he'd hear me, but what the hell. "Goddammit!" I hissed as Harley took another curve way too fast.

He was going to wipe out. Even on my Tomahawk with four fucking wheels, I had to navigate them more slowly. The back end of Harley's motorcycle fishtailed and then the bike slid, taking Harley down with it. My heart stopped in my chest as the bike slid across the Seventeen, heading right for the guardrail.

Metal crunched as the bike met the guardrail and I heard the distinct sound of Harley's scream. His hand flew out, grabbing the jagged metal of the rail before he flew over the side. The motorcycle took flight over the drop. I came to a squealing stop and dumped my bike, running after Harley who was hanging precariously over the edge.

"Harley!" I shouted. "Hang on!"

"Achilles?! Help me!"

I ran to him, throwing my body forward as Harley lost his grip. I grabbed his wrist and Harley shouted in pain. I wrapped my other hand around his bicep and hauled him up and into my lap. I pulled his helmet off carefully.

"Are you all right?" I asked, panicked.

"My hand hurts, and I think I broke my leg," Harley sobbed. "Holden's bike…it's gone."

"Fuck the bike!" I snarled. "Dammit! You could have *died*! What the fuck were you thinking?" I assessed Harley quickly. The metal of the guardrail had cut through his leather jacket. I removed it carefully and tried to get a good look at Harley's wound. I whipped off my jacket and then took off my shirt. Ripping off the bottom of the shirt, I wrapped it around Harley's arm. I tried to get a good look at his leg, but it was too dark. I felt around, trying to feel if there was a break.

"Fuck!" Harley stiffened as I ran my hand over his shin.

"Don't move!" I ordered. I called the police and kept Harley close to me. He was shivering and probably going into shock. I alerted the police to where we were and then wrapped my jacket around Harley's trembling frame.

"They're coming," I assured him.

"Holden's b-b-bike," Harley chattered.

"I'm sure we can get it back," I said soothingly.

"They're going to be so mad at me." Harley sobbed in my arms.

"The bike can be replaced, Harley. You can't."

"They won't care," he whispered.

"I fucking care!" I held his chin up and searched his eyes. "I care!"

Harley's bloodshot eyes met mine and I wanted to kiss him so badly in that moment, to let him know that someone fucking cared if he lived or died. I wanted to strangle his parents with my bare hands! Sirens sounded in the distance and I pulled Harley into my body heat. His whole body racked with sobs and I did my best to soothe him. He was still babbling about the bike when an ambulance pulled up next to us, followed by a fire truck and a tow truck. The EMTs approached me and I stood up, holding Harley in my arms.

"Sir? We're going to need you to let go." One of them motioned to Harley.

I relinquished Harley, but kept my eyes on him as the police and firemen cordoned off our lane of traffic. The tow truck driver was looking over the side of the cliff.

"Hey, the bike is stuck on a rock," he exclaimed.

I peered over the side. "Make sure you get it. Hear me?"

"Sir? Is that your bike over there?" One of the firemen pointed to my Tomahawk.

"Yeah, can you put it on the tow truck?" I asked the driver. "I'm riding in the ambulance."

"That is one gorgeous piece of equipment." The driver whistled.

I narrowed my eyes and pinned him with a look. "Get both bikes. Don't worry, you'll get paid plenty. Take it to Roy's Auto in Flagstaff." I got the tow truck driver's card and then climbed into the ambulance and sat down. Harley was lying motionless, his eyes closed as his chest rose and fell slowly.

"What did you give him?" I asked, worried.

"Just a little something to calm him down," the EMT assured me. "He's got a nasty gash in his upper arm, some road rash, but he's lucky to be alive. Someone up there must like this kid."

As the ambulance drove us back to Flagstaff's hospital, I called everyone I could think of. Stan was first on that list. As their manager, he needed to be privy to anything. I also called Rebel, Ransom and Gareth. Ransom assured me that he would get in touch with Harley's parents. I wasn't sure that was such a good idea. Harley was taken back to a private emergency exam room as I paced the hallway. I should have been faster. I should have stopped him. I should have done a lot of things. I grasped at my hair and let out a frustrated shout.

"Whoa!" Ransom stepped back from me. "Is Harley okay?"

I hadn't even realized he was there. I sighed audibly and met Ransom's eyes.

"He's got damage to his arm and some road rash on his thighs and shin."

"What was he doing?" Ransom rubbed his face with his hands.

"Driving like a maniac."

"Oh God." Ransom sunk into a chair.

The ER doors whooshed open and Rebel ran in with Gareth and Axel.

"Is he okay?" Gareth almost shouted.

I explained again to Rebel and Gareth what I knew. Stan arrived and then they all filled him in. I sat down and stared at the tiles of the emergency room floor.

"You were following him?" Gareth asked me.

"Yeah, I was less than a mile behind him on my bike. He should have never taken the bike as angry as he was."

"What do you mean?" Gareth's brows furrowed. "Where is he?!"

I looked up to see Harley's father speaking with a nurse. His face was beet red and he was wringing his hands. I stood up and walked over to the nurse's station.

"He's in the back. They're looking him over now."

I was pulled away by my bicep and was surprised to find Axel staring me down.

"Let's talk," he ordered.

I followed Axel to the vending machines and he turned to look at me. I met his eyes because, dammit, I'd done my best to make sure Harley never got hurt.

"What?" I snapped. "I was right behind him!"

"What set him off, Axel? Why was Harley riding a motorcycle in this weather?"

"It's a long story, and I don't feel like rehashing it. Harley blew out of that garage full throttle and it was just luck that I caught up to him. He almost went over, Axel! He would have if I hadn't gotten there in time."

"I'm sorry," Axel blew out a breath. "When Gareth gets panicked, it seems to rub off on me. I know you'd give your life to protect Harley's."

"Fucking right I would."

Axel clapped me on the back and pulled me into a half hug. I was getting used to it now. Somehow, Gareth had rubbed off on Axel the killer. He was a bit softer. I couldn't say shit. Harley was rubbing off on me. We walked back to the waiting room and I noticed Harley's father was gone.

"Where's Harley's dad?" I asked.

Gareth pointed down the hall. "He demanded to see his son."

"Ha! *Now* he has a son?" I snarled.

Shouting came from down the hall and then the unmistakable sound of Harley's devastated voice floated out to me. I ran through a hallway full of people, pushing them out of the way. I slammed through the door and found Harley on the floor on his knees.

"Get out!" I ground out at Harley's father through gritted teeth.

"Excuse me? You have no right to tell me what to do!"

"Get. Out! Harley doesn't need this right now!" I shouted

"Security!"

"Oh yes, please call them." I leaned into his face. "It's about to get ugly."

Two men came from behind and tried to subdue me. I fought them both off and two more arrived. Harley was still on the floor, sobbing about how sorry he was, and a rage came over me I hadn't felt since I was deployed.

"STOP!" Axel roared. "Let him go or you'll be dealing with us." Axel motioned to Hammer and Buster behind him. "And we don't fight fair."

"Mr. Payne," Gareth stepped in between the chaos. "Please, just go home. This isn't helping Harley."

"He took my son's motorcycle and wrecked it! He had no business —"

"Get out," Gareth said forcefully. "We will take care of Harley. Don't worry, I'm sure the bike can be fixed."

I got a death glare from Harley's father before he huffed and left the room. The security guards holding me let go and I moved to Harley's side.

"Hey," I said softly. "Are you okay? Do you need help getting up?"

"I told you," Harley whispered. "I told you he'd be mad."

"You need to be in bed." I placed an arm under him and helped him up, carefully placing him in bed. I noticed a red mark on Harley's face and balled my fists. "Did he hit you?"

"He was mad, he didn't mean it —"

A roar escaped me and then I was blasting past everyone in the room, my mission to find Harley's father front and center. A hand clasped over my bicep and I was whipped back. I expected to see Axel, but turned to find Hammer's icy-blue eyes staring into mine.

"Don't." He shook his head.

"Don't?" I asked incredulously. "He *hit* him! The guy was in an almost fatal accident and his father hit him! He doesn't even give a shit about his son, just the damn motorcycle! Give me one good reason why I shouldn't hunt that fucker down and kill him."

"Harley needs you." Hammer motioned with his chin to Harley's room. Harley was curled up on the bed in the fetal position and Gareth was trying to soothe him. "You, Achilles, and no one else right now."

I sighed and my shoulders slumped. I knew Hammer was right. Harley had grown accustomed to me being there, and I had grown accustomed to him. I patted Hammer's bicep and moved toward the room. Harley lifted his head as I walked back in and the smallest of smiles graced his lips.

"You came back," he whispered.

"Yeah, and I'm not leaving."

I stayed with Harley overnight. The doctors wanted to keep him under observation for a full twenty-four hours. Thank God he'd been wearing a helmet. His arm had been stitched up and I was assured he'd have no lasting effects from the injury. His legs had been cleaned and wrapped. I watched as he slept peacefully. After everything he'd been through, I wanted to protect him from anything else.

"Hey."

I glanced over my shoulder at Gareth behind me. He stepped into the room and leaned over Harley, caressing his cheek. I knew these guys would bleed for one another. They were all like brothers and I respected the hell out of them for their loyalty.

"I told Jinx not to come," Gareth whispered. "I told him Harley was okay."

"Let me guess — that went over really well, right?"

"He's on his way," Gareth chuckled.

My cell vibrated in my back pocket and I fished it out, looking at the number.

"I have to take this. Be right back."

I stepped outside and took the call. My mother's voice came over the line.

"Achilles."

"Hey, Mama. How are you?"

"Your father is not doing so good. He would like to see you."

I looked back at the emergency room doors. Shit. I couldn't leave Harley, but there was no way I wasn't going to see my father.

"I'll be there, Mama. Just give me a few days. I'll be coming with Harley."

"Oh, I would very much like to meet this man. You make him sound very funny."

"Oh, yeah, he's a barrel of laughs, Mama."

"I am looking forward to seeing you. So is your father."

"I'll see you soon. I'll send you all the info as soon as I know what day and time. Love you, Mama."

"Love you, Achilles."

I hung up and groaned, staring up at the night sky. This wouldn't be easy. Harley was as stubborn as a fucking mule. He needed to get the fuck out of Dodge for a while; and after his accident, I knew I could talk Stan and the guys into letting me take him. My mother would dote on him and my father would keep him busy. Now I just had to figure out how I was going to get him to come with me. I headed back into the hospital and into Harley's room. A nurse was checking his IV bag and his vitals. Harley was out, sleeping peacefully.

"Did you give him something?" I asked the nurse.

"Yes, we gave him a mild sedative after the 'incident.'" She used her fingers to imply invisible quotation marks. "He was extremely upset."

"Yeah, I got that." I nodded, taking Harley's hand.

"Are you his boyfriend?" she asked.

Gareth snickered in the chair next to the bed and I shot him a look.

"I'm his bodyguard," I informed her.

"Lucky guy." She winked as she left.

"The way you acted, I'd have thought you were his boyfriend, too." Gareth reclined in the chair with a yawn.

"He scared the shit out of me. Rebel and I were talking about Holden, how we knew he'd have left Harley a letter. According to Harley, his parents never gave him one. I know for a fact Holden would have written one. We all have to in case we die."

"I agree, Holden would have written a letter."

We both turned to see Jinx in the doorway. He walked over to the bed and caressed Harley's cheek.

"There's no way in hell Holden wouldn't have written Harley a goodbye letter. They were as close as Gareth and Ransom." Jinx sighed and sat on the edge of the bed. "Those fucking assholes."

"I need to take Harley out of here," I announced. "I'm going to Greece to see my parents, I want to take Harley with me."

"I think it's a good idea." Gareth nodded. "Get him out of here for a bit."

"He could have died tonight," Jinx said, his voice a little shaky. "What the fuck was he thinking?" Jinx leaned in to Harley's ear. "Don't do that shit again."

"How long are you here, Jinx?" I asked.

"As long as he needs me. London Boys are wrapping up their tour, but if you're taking him to Greece, I'll go back to be with Jayden. You'll take good care of Harley, right?"

"Don't I always?"

Jinx turned to look at me. "I trust you, Achilles. Do what's best for Harley."

"I intend to."

~*~

By late afternoon, the doctor was releasing Harley. He looked a little banged up, but he was walking on his own. I still held him around his waist as I helped him into the waiting wheelchair. He gave me the stink eye as he sat down.

"Not my rules," I explained.

I hadn't talked to him about leaving with me yet. I wanted to get him home before we sat down and talked about it. My truck was waiting out front as I wheeled Harley out of the hospital. I helped him in and then shut his door, turning to find the nurse there with a smile and a bag of Harley's belongings.

"You take good care of our guy, yes?" She grinned.

"Of course." I took the bag and gave her my best smile.

Harley was looking out the passenger window as I got in and pulled out of the hospital. After five minutes of silence on the drive, I finally couldn't take it anymore.

"Harley?"

"Hmm?"

"Are you okay?"

"Oh yeah, sure. I busted my brother's motorcycle and ended up in the E.R. where my dad went bat shit crazy and slapped me. I'm all good."

"Holden's motorcycle is not busted. I had it sent to a garage. It will be perfect when they're done with it."

"Yeah, right," Harley snorted.

"Don't you trust me, Harley?"

Harley turned in the seat to look at me. I glanced over at him and was shocked to see a look of anger on his face.

"Of course I trust you! You saved my life!"

"Good. Now, shush," I chuckled.

"Excuse me?" Harley narrowed his gaze.

I pulled into Harley's driveway and cut the engine. Harley was out the passenger door before I could even shut mine. I followed him up the walk and waited patiently for him to unlock the front door.

My eyes strayed to the living room window and I grabbed Harley's bicep.

"What the —" he began.

I placed a finger over my lips and pointed to the window. Harley looked back at me in shock and I pulled him behind me, removing my gun from the waistband of my jeans. I motioned to him to give me the keys and I unlocked the door, keeping Harley behind me as I entered. I left the lights off and peered around the semi-lit house. Everything was quiet, but the ripped screen on the front window did not make me comfortable. I dragged Harley to his room and shut the door. After checking the closet, under the bed, and anywhere else someone could hide, I threw Harley his suitcase.

"Stay in this room and pack," I said quietly. "I'm going to check the rest of the house. Lock the door behind me."

"Wait, what if someone's out there?" Harley whispered.

I showed him my gun and Harley's eyes widened.

"Stay put!" I ordered.

I did a thorough check of the rest of the house, but didn't find anything. Nothing was even out of place or missing. The window was cracked open just enough to get a finger through and I shut it and locked it before going back to Harley's room. I knocked softly.

"It's me."

Harley let me in and I shut and locked the door behind me. He was packing his clothes into his suitcase just like I'd asked him to.

"Where are we going?" Harley asked.

"Greece."

"Isn't that a little far? I mean, a ripped window screen doesn't call for a trip across the Atlantic."

"Just finish packing, we're going to my house tonight and we'll leave in the morning." Harley stood there with his mouth hanging open and I sighed in frustration. "What?"

"What's really going on?" Harley sat down on the bed.

"Look, I wanted to talk to you about this anyway. My dad isn't doing so well and I would like it if you came to Greece with me."

Harley looked down at his lap and wrung his hands. I sat down next to him and playfully shoved his shoulder.

"What is it?" I asked. He mumbled under his breath and I leaned in closer. "What?"

"I don't like to fly," he mumbled.

Well, that was interesting.

"But you fly all the time on your tours," I pointed out.

"Well, I'm usually asleep when I fly. I take, um, stuff to knock me out."

"Okay, so you'll take it. Are you afraid of flying?"

"I'm afraid of crashing." Harley peered up at me through his lashes. "You're not going to make fun of me?"

"Why would I do that? There's nothing wrong with how you feel. You're not the only one, I'm sure. You can pack your coloring books if you want. That will help too, right?"

"Yeah, I guess. I want to bring my guitar."

"That's fine. You need help?"

"Nope." Harley stood up and then looked down at me. "Thanks, ya know? For everything."

"I was afraid you wouldn't want to go to Greece," I admitted.

"Who doesn't want to go to Greece? I'll just make sure I bring my pills."

I helped Harley pack the rest of his things and then opened the door slowly. I peeked out into the house and moved forward, keeping Harley behind me. We left the house and I made sure I locked the front door. I kept my eyes on the neighborhood as I helped Harley into my truck. Once we pulled away, I relaxed a bit. I was going to have to call Axel and have his guys do a sweep of Harley's house. I had no idea if someone had broken in or not. Harley had some fans, but deranged? I wasn't so sure.

I pulled up to my house and realized both Hammer and Buster were home. This should be fun. I helped Harley with his bags and walked behind him as we headed to the front door.

"So this is where you guys live, huh?" Harley looked around appreciatively.

"Yes, for now. Eventually, we'll buy our own place."

I unlocked the door and ushered Harley in. A sinful smell was emanating from the kitchen and I headed in that direction with Harley close on my heels. I stepped into the kitchen to see Hammer in his apron cooking what looked to be spaghetti. Buster was at the table working a crossword puzzle. I cleared my throat and they turned to look at me.

"Guys, we have a guest for tonight." Both Hammer and Buster nodded and I turned to Harley. "Why don't you get set up in my room, okay? Come on out when you're done and you can eat. It's at the end of the hall on your right."

"Okay." Harley nodded. "Thanks."

Harley left and I checked to make sure he was down the hall before turning back to Hammer and Buster.

"I think someone broke into his house. Can you guys go over there after we're gone? I'm taking Harley to Greece."

"Does he know about your fear of flying?" Buster cocked a brow.

"Shut up."

I stepped into Achilles' bedroom and dropped my bag. Scenes of Greece were everywhere. A breath-taking picture of the Temple of Aphaia took up most of one wall and the Acropolis of Athens took up another. Right in the middle, above Achilles' bed, was a picture of the New York skyline. I tilted my head, studying it. It seemed odd amongst Greek photos. I shrugged and headed back to the kitchen. Low voices met my ears and I crept up the hall silently. I could make out three distinctive voices; two were extremely deep. My mouth dropped as I realized Hammer and Buster were talking. I jumped into the kitchen and pointed at them.

"Ah HA! You *do* talk!"

Hammer folded his arms across his chest and gave me a pointed look. "We'll deny it." He turned back to the stove.

"Holy shit," I whispered.

"He is a lot to take in, eh?" Buster got up and pulled a chair out for me. "Don't mind the Santa apron."

"Fuck off, Kirk," Hammer threw over his shoulder.

"Kirk, huh?" I grinned as I took the seat Buster offered.

"Yes, and that guy over there," Buster pointed to Hammer. "Is Marcello Balboni."

"Gareth said he thought you were Italian," I chuckled.

"I'm Kirk Kendrick, and you know Achilles."

"What's your last name, Achilles?" I asked.

"Castellanos," Hammer answered for him.

He put a plate in front of me and my mouth watered. "What is this?"

"Spaghetti with Italian sausage, onion and green peppers."

"Marc here is the cook for us," Achilles said as he dug into his own plate.

"Yes, although I know Achilles can cook. Kirk burns water."

"I do not. I can make that noodle shit."

My head was ping-ponging between the bodyguards. I was still in shock that they actually spoke in my presence. I kind of felt, I don't know, honored? The three of them dwarfed their little round kitchen table. I felt closed in, like I was in some weird Tetris game.

"So, Achilles tells us you're going to Greece with him," Buster mentioned between mouthfuls of food.

"That's what he says." I shrugged.

"I think it will be nice for Harley to get away for a while. Let his wounds heal." Achilles leaned into me, eyeing my arm. "Feel better?"

"It's okay, kind of itchy," I admitted.

"Stitches will do that," Buster agreed. "Good thing it wasn't worse."

"Well, my guardian angel was looking out for me." I glanced up at Achilles.

"And I always will." Achilles touched my arm carefully.

I was certain every sound in the room stopped. I glanced at Hammer and Buster and found them staring at us. Achilles cleared his throat and went back to eating. I lowered my head and began to eat. The spaghetti was fucking awesome! I hadn't had food like that in a long time.

"This is really good, Hamm — um, Marc? What should I call you?"

"Asshole suits him well," Buster chuckled.

"Well, you can call me Marc while you're here. Unless you prefer Hammer."

"I get the nickname." I motioned to Hammer. "But you?" I pointed to Buster. "Not so sure about."

"I'm the one they call in when something needs to be busted." Buster grinned, twirling his fork in his fingers.

"Why don't you have a nickname?" I glanced over at Achilles.

"Oh, he does, he just doesn't like it," Hammer answered.

Achilles seemed to stiffen next to me and I searched his face.

"Why don't you like it?"

"Thanatos," Achilles said quietly. "The Greek god of death."

Huh, I was going to have to look that one up.

"Achilles could take a guy out from over a mile away," Hammer continued. "Still can, actually."

"Like I said, you and Rebel need to hang out." I tried to smile at Achilles, but he wouldn't make eye contact with me.

"Well! I'm stuffed." Buster pushed away from the table. "If I don't see you in the morning, have a great flight and enjoy Greece, Harley."

I shook Buster's hand and gave him a grin. "Don't worry, I won't tell the others you guys actually speak."

Hammer grunted at me and Buster gave me a nod before placing his dishes in the dishwasher. Hammer excused himself as well, and that left a silent Achilles and me.

"Why are you so quiet all of a sudden?" I asked.

"It's nothing."

I turned in the seat to face him and gripped his chin, pulling his face around to mine.

"That's a load of shit. Talk to me."

"I just don't like talking about who I was, or still am."

"Because you think I'll somehow look at you differently? We went over this in my backyard." Achilles cast his eyes downward and I lifted his chin higher. "Look at me."

Those gray eyes met mine and I saw pain etched in them. I didn't understand why Achilles felt the way he did. I looked at him and all I saw was a guy who put up with my shit, carried me home when I'd had too much to drink, and who had always been right at my side when I needed him. Damn, he had gorgeous lips; plump bottom lip and a hair away from a Cupid's bow, not to mention that sexy stubble across his upper lip and jawline. I blinked and realized I was staring at his lips. I lifted my eyes to find mirth in his. I coughed and sat back in my chair, releasing his chin.

"You are one hell of a guy, Achilles Castellanos, and don't you ever forget it."

"Yes, sir." Achilles chuckled.

"Now eat up. We have a long flight tomorrow."

After cleaning up, Achilles escorted me back to his room and made sure I knew where everything was. When I asked him where he was going to sleep, he merely shrugged and bid me goodnight. I laid there, in his bed, imagining what it would be like to be with him. The more time I spent with Achilles, the more I wanted him. He was so much more than a soldier or bodyguard. He genuinely cared for all of us. Jinx told me that Achilles had gone off on him in California. I didn't really believe it until now. I remembered the night of the crash, how he yelled at me on the side of the road. He said he cared.

I rolled to my side and sighed. I vaguely remembered he and my father getting into it, the security guards trying to remove Achilles from my room and the fight that ensued. How anyone would be stupid enough to go up against Achilles was beyond me. Even after he went after my father, he came back less than two minutes later. I'd never been so happy to see him. Achilles was becoming a solid fixture in my life, and I realized I was starting to have inappropriate feelings for him. The guy was straight and just watching out for me.

I needed to reel in how I was feeling before he walked out of my life, too. And then I would be alone.

Again.

~*~

Morning came all too soon. Achilles had us packed and ready for the airport. The band's Gulfstream jet was waiting for us as we entered the airport. Achilles and I walked out onto the tarmac and he seemed to flinch as the doors to the jet opened. We climbed up the stairs and got settled into the plush couches in the main cabin. Achilles fastened his seat belt and stared at his hands as the jet began to turn around and head for the runway.

"Achilles?" I sat forward.

"Yes?"

"Are you okay?"

"I thought you were going to take your pills?"

"I will, as soon as we get up in the air and I get a drink. What's wrong?"

"We have a little more in common than you thought."

"Oh?"

"I hate crashing, too."

I lifted my hand to my mouth to cover my grin. I took Achilles' hand in mine and forced him to look up at me. "Why didn't you say anything when I told you?"

"Because then you'd think I was only saying it to placate you."

"That's true. Are you going to be okay?"

"Could I...color while you sleep?"

"Sure." I reached into my bag and dragged out my coloring books and crayons. Achilles took them with a shaky hand as the jet's nose lifted and we were airborne. I squashed the feeling of sickness I got at takeoff and concentrated on trying to make Achilles more comfortable.

"I could stay awake? We could color together, if you want?"

"I don't want you to stress out, you've had enough stress in your life already without adding me and my phobias."

"How 'bout we color for a bit and then I'll take my pills. Sound good?"

"Okay, sure." Achilles nodded.

I noticed he looked a little green. "I don't think I remember you looking like this on our tour in Europe."

"Because you were crashed out and I was in front with Axel," Achilles pointed out.

"Ah." I nodded. "Okay, well, let's get you set up with a book. Which one?" I held up two coloring books, one with a jungle theme and another with different breeds of dogs.

"The jungle one."

"Jungle one it is." I placed the box of crayons down on the table in front of us and began tracing along the inner line of my picture.

"Hey, Harley?"

"Yeah?"

"Thanks for this. I'm supposed to be the strong one watching out for you, but sometimes it feels like it's the other way around."

"I like to think we watch out for each other." I winked at him.

Achilles smiled and ducked his head, working on his coloring book. I couldn't help but notice the way he bit his bottom lip in concentration. It was so cute. He had long, slender fingers, but they held a plethora of scars, which only made his hands sexier. We ended up seated side-by-side, coloring and chatting about Greece and what Achilles loved about it. The food seemed to be number one on his list. I yawned and stretched my arms out. I hadn't even taken a pill and I was sleepy. My eyelids drooped and a goofy smile split my lips as I watched Achilles coloring like a madman.

"Get some rest, Harley," Achilles said from far away.

I closed my eyes and that was it.

~*~

I woke up some time later with my head on Achilles' shoulder. He was sleeping with a crayon in his hand. I removed it slowly and placed it back in the box. He looked at peace just then, and I didn't want to wake him. I peeked out the window. A full moon was out and we were flying above the clouds. Everything seemed so peaceful up here, with the stars twinkling in the night. I pressed my hand to the window and thought about Holden. I knew he was up there, hopefully hanging out with his friends who had died. I wondered if Achilles ever looked at the night sky and thought the same way I did.

Achilles stirred in his sleep and I took that time to study him. His hands were twice the size of mine, and his shoulders were broad. He had long legs and a narrow waist, but his chest, even clothed, was impressive. I loved his ink. I peered closer at a tattoo on his inner wrist. It was a sword with the word Thanatos inked underneath it. I really needed to check into Greek mythology. I was so involved in checking out his tattoo, I hadn't realized he'd woken up.

"Hey," Achilles said sleepily.

"Hi. I guess we were both tired, huh?"

"Yeah, I'm going to go up front and see how much longer the flight is. Are you thirsty?"

"I am actually, and hungry."

"Well, looks like we'll have food in a second." Achilles pointed to the flight attendant coming our way. "Be right back."

Achilles walked towards the cockpit and I smiled at the woman who was carrying drinks.

"Hey, Grace. Sorry to drag you last minute." When Axel had come on as our security, he hired the attendants for our jet. Turned out Grace was a good friend of Mac's wife, Christy.

"Are you kidding me? I love Greece!" she practically squealed. "When Christy asked if I wanted to work on a private jet versus commercial, I thought she was shitting me."

"Well, the guys love you, so you'll always have a job." I smiled as she handed me a soda.

"So, you and Achilles, eh?" Grace gave me a wicked grin.

"Oh no, nothing like that. He's just my bodyguard."

"Did someone tell him that?" Grace giggled.

"What does that mean?"

Achilles' return from the cockpit interrupted us. He looked from me to Grace, and then back.

"Should I come back?" he asked.

"Um, no. Why?" I stood up and motioned for him to sit down. "I'll be back. I have to hit the head."

"Okay. Pilot says we've got eight more hours."

"Ugh." I trudged off to the bathroom.

We ate, then ended up playing cards and watching a movie. Before I knew it, we were touching down in Athens. The sun was just rising as we exited the airport. A tall man in a suit was holding a sign that said "Castellanos" and Achilles headed his way.

"Titus!" Achilles called out.

The older gentleman's face broke out into a smile as he spotted Achilles. They hugged and I stood off to the side, nervously looking around.

"Titus, this is Harley Payne. Harley, this is Titus. He's been with my family for years."

The man pulled me into a hug and kissed my cheeks. I was a bit startled by it all, but I felt immediately at home. We ended up in a stretch limo and Achilles sat across from me, staring out the window.

"So, where do your parents live?" I asked.

"On the Island of Aegina. The Temple of Aphaia is there. I'll take you if you want."

"An island? Meaning we're going to get on a boat?"

"Well, we could swim there, but the water is pretty frigid right now." Achilles chuckled.

"Funny." I stared at him.

"Do you get sea sick?"

"No, I'll be okay."

We ended up taking a hydrofoil ferry across to the island. I stood on the deck, lifting my face to the sun. It was in the lower seventies, and the crisp air brought with it the smells of the sea. I already loved it and we hadn't even gotten to the island yet. Achilles was at the bow, watching the waves as we sliced through the water. I joined him and marveled at the amount of fishing boats on the water.

"What is that?" I pointed ahead of us.

"That's the temple of Apollo. I can take you there, too."

"Wow, that's so awesome that you live so close to temples."

"See that over there? That's ancient Aegina. Aegina was said to be named after the nymph, Aegina, daughter of the river god, Asopus. Zeus seduced her and took over the island, renaming it Oenone. Aegina gave birth to Aeacus; he was the first king of the island and grandfather to Achilles. Aeacus renamed the island Aegina for his mother."

"Wow, you know a lot about this stuff," I said in awe.

"I've spent a lot of time here."

"Will you tell me more?"

"Of course. You really want to hear about all this boring stuff?"

"It's not boring to me." I smiled.

"Aegina was also the first to mint coins. I have one at my parents' house. It has a turtle on it."

"I look forward to seeing it," I said sincerely.

I really was in awe of everything around me. It was boring to sit in class and look at pictures and hear the stories, but to actually be here and get to see it close up? Fantastic. Plus, I had one hell of a hot guide. I snickered and Achilles glanced over at me. I shrugged and watched the island get closer.

Once we docked, another car was waiting for us. The streets were narrow, and everywhere you looked, houses lined the beach. It was breathtakingly beautiful and I couldn't stop staring. The car turned into a narrow drive and a white house appeared behind a mass of greenery. Light blue shutters were open, as were the windows, allowing the sea breeze to gently blow the curtains.

The car came to a stop in front, and a couple emerged from the house holding hands. I could see immediately where Achilles got his looks. The woman was absolutely beautiful, with blonde hair that flowed over her shoulders. The man at her side was much taller than her; he also had blond hair and was massive. Achilles got out of the car and approached them, arms open wide.

"Achilles!" the woman shrieked.

I exited the car and held back a bit, not sure what I was supposed to do. Achilles turned to me and held out a hand.

"Mama, Papa, this is Harley."

I slipped my hand into his and he pulled me forward. The woman held my face in her hands, looking at me with a smile. "I am Callidora, but you may call me Calli. This is my husband, Krios. We are so happy to have you, Harley."

"Thank you. I'm very happy to be here. It's so beautiful."

"Well, come inside. We've made lunch for you." Calli gestured to the house.

"Let me help Titus get the luggage, Mama." Achilles turned back to the car and I followed him like a lost puppy. I grabbed one of my bags and Achilles grabbed most of the others. Titus placed his hands on his hips and glared at Achilles.

"I am not so old, Achilles," he argued.

"Oh, I know. I just want you to rest up before I kick your butt in video games." Achilles winked.

"I have been practicing." Titus grinned. "Maybe Harley can beat you."

"What game are we talking about?" I asked.

"You'll see."

I followed them back up the walk and into the house. I almost gasped out loud at the vision in front of me. Marble floors led in all directions and a giant crystal chandelier hung in the front foyer. A small, round table was beneath it, displaying a large vase overflowing with exotic flowers. Everywhere on the walls were paintings and pictures from all eras. A staircase was right in front of me and it wound up and around to the second floor. These people had money. And a lot of it.

"Follow me, Harley." Achilles seemed to notice the way I was looking around and smiled. "You have questions?"

"So many." I nodded.

"Come on." Achilles laughed.

Chapter 9

Achilles

I showed Harley his room. He seemed to stand in the middle of it for a very long time before he spoke. I knew my parents' house was a lot to take in, but they had never really overdone it in my opinion. The house was tasteful, beautifully decorated and in prime condition

"This is…wow," Harley said slowly. "The house is made of stone on the outside?"

"Traditional stone, yes. There are two verandas, one with a panoramic view, and a courtyard below us with flowers. There's a path to the beach I can show you later. Are you hungry? My mom made food."

"I could eat." Harley rummaged through his bag and pulled out some clothes. "Can I get cleaned up a little? I can meet you down there."

"Sure. I'll just," I thumbed behind me. "Be down there."

I took the stairs back down and headed for the kitchen. My mother was at the stove and my father was seated at the table. I could smell the lamb cooking and peeked into the pot. I inhaled and licked my lips.

"I missed this." I wrapped my arms around my mom.

"It is so good to see you, Achilles. We have missed you."

"I know I haven't come around as much, and I'm sorry about that. This new job has me busy 24/7." I turned to my father and took his hands. They were shaking a little, but not as bad as they used to, though.

"Papa, how did the surgery work? Things are better?"

My father had gone through so much already due to his Parkinson's disease. So far, he'd had the deep brain stimulation, pallidotomy and thalamotomy, each procedure draining him. Now he was going to try the experimental one. Neurotransplantation.

"I am better. Please, tell me all about your job with the rock band."

I sat down and took his hand, kissing it. "They are a great bunch of guys, Papa. They love each other and would do anything for each other. The guys I work with, I feel like I'm back on a team again. I feel like I have purpose."

"Would Harley have anything to do with that?" My mother grinned at me.

"You would be angry if I told you Harley's story." I sighed, shaking my head.

My mother spoke in Greek and my head snapped up.

"It's not like that. Well, at least not for him, okay?"

"Oh, Achilles. I just want you to find love." My mother took my face in her hands. "You were broken, but you are whole now. I would very much like to see you happy with someone."

"This is my job, okay? That's all it is," I protested. The last thing I needed was my mother trying to set me up with Harley. Yeah, because that would happen. Harley was straight and even though he had kissed me, I knew it was because he was drunk. A slight cough came from behind me and I turned to find Harley in the doorway. He was shifting from one foot to the other.

"Come in!" My mother dragged Harley in and sat him down at the table. "Do you like Greek food?"

"Oh yes. I had some last time we were here on tour." Harley nodded.

"Don't give him any ouzo, Mama." I pointed at her and tried to look stern.

Harley snickered and I leveled a glare at him.

"You like ouzo?" my mother asked Harley.

"Well, I like what I remember of it."

"I made baklava for dessert. Did you have any of that?" she asked.

"Um, I don't know." Harley bit at his bottom lip.

"Well, you will have it today." My mother palmed his cheek.

I smiled at the look on Harley's face. His cheeks were lightly dusted with pink as my mother planted a kiss on the top of his head. I knew he wasn't used to the attention, since his own parents were sorely lacking in any tenderness. Hell, ANY emotion. My father chatted up Harley right away, asking him if he'd play a song while we were visiting. Harley of course agreed, which put a smile on my father's face. I missed seeing that. With all the pain he'd gone through, he really needed some light in his life. Harley brought light to anyone he touched. As much as he felt invisible, or unloved, his mere presence lightened up any room. My father got into the story of how he met my mom and how he made his fortune.

"Here, we live off the land and the sea. I lost my parents young and then I met Callidora in the market place, shopping for her family. I fell in love with her the instant our eyes met. I was just a fisherman, not good enough for someone like her."

"Stop it, Krios." My mother swatted his arm playfully.

"I decided then, if I was to woo her, I would need to have something to give her. It was then that I designed an idea for a shoe that fishermen could wear. It could be worn in the water and have grip on the bottom to stop them from slipping on the rocks. It grew from there. I designed pants, shirts, jackets, and now we sell them all over in the fishing industry."

"Yes, he has made quite the fortune." My mother nodded in agreement. "We moved to New York and sold his line there as well. Then we had Achilles. When my parents were killed, we came home to run their restaurant. Now we hire people to keep it running."

"Wow." Harley was awestruck. "That's pretty impressive."

"Achilles joined the Army and we have stayed here in the house Krios grew up in. Over the years, we have added to it, but when we are gone, it will belong to Achilles." My mother caressed my cheek.

"And I will keep it in the family," I vowed.

"Well, I love it here already. It's so gorgeous and you can hear and smell the sea," Harley marveled.

"Let us get you fed, eh?" My mother mussed my hair. "Maybe you can take Harley for a walk along the beach after dinner?"

I narrowed my gaze at my mother. She was still going to try to hook me up whether I wanted it or not. Looking at Harley, I definitely wanted it, but I knew he didn't want me like that. No matter what his past behavior had shown. I'd never seen him with a man, only women.

Harley ate like a man possessed. He had seconds of lamb and potatoes, and three helpings of baklava. I kept him away from the ouzo and made sure he had plenty of water. We helped my mother clean up and my father bid us goodnight. I kissed his cheek and hugged him.

"No matter what you think, Achilles, that man cares for you," he murmured in my ear.

I squeezed him tight and gave him a smile as he headed up the stairs. Harley appeared beside me and looked up at me with wonder.

"What?" I asked.

"You look so much like him. Even his eyes."

"Thank you. You look really tired," I observed.

"I really am. Rain check on the walk?"

"Sure. Sleep well, Harley."

I watched him walk up the stairs. I glanced to my side to see my mother staring after Harley. She came over next to me and took my hand.

"He is in pain."

"Yeah, Mama, he really is."

"Tell me."

My mother and I went out onto the veranda on the back side of the house. We had a view of Apollo's temple and a beautiful full moon. I didn't even know where to start when it came to Harley.

"He has lost someone close to him," my mother guessed, breaking the silence.

"Yes. His brother. I wish that was the only thing that was hurting him right now."

I told my mother the whole story — well, what all I knew. She listened intently, never interrupting, but I could see the anger flare in her eyes. I never wanted for affection when I was younger. My parents acted as if I was a gift from the gods. I wrapped up the story and waited for her to speak.

"I will take him with me in the morning," she announced.

"What? Where?"

"Don't worry." My mother grinned knowingly. "I will bring him back to you."

"Mama," I sighed in frustration. "Stop trying to set me up. Harley does not think of me in that way."

"Look at you. You are strong, kind, caring, and beautiful! What man wouldn't want you? What woman, for that matter?"

"You're biased." I pointed at her.

"Go look in the mirror, Achilles. We named you properly. Maybe Harley is your lobster?"

"What?"

"Oh yes! I watched a TV show a while back and they talked about how lobsters mated for life."

I laughed. "Goodnight, Mama."

She kissed my cheeks and stared into my eyes. "It is time for you to love again, Achilles. I believe you and Harley need each other."

"The only thing I can be to him is a friend." I put my hand up to stop my mother's next words. "He doesn't feel that way about me, okay? Stop trying to make it happen. I love you." I hugged her and headed up the stairs.

I passed by Harley's room and saw him in bed with an e-reader. I knocked and he looked up.

"Hey." Harley smiled.

"Couldn't sleep?" I asked.

"I wanted to finish this chapter. Jayden turned me onto these books about assassin werewolves."

I cocked a brow and Harley laughed. "I know, I had the same look."

"Well, goodnight, Harley."

"Night."

I closed his door and headed to my room. My parents had kept it the same — my sport trophies lined one shelf of my built-in bookcase. I thumbed through some of my old books and stared at the white envelope sitting between my two Greek history books. I shook my head and got in the shower, washing off the trip. I fell into bed and stared at the ceiling. The sea breeze blew through the window and I exhaled slowly, letting the sounds of the sea lull me to sleep.

~*~

I woke up to the sounds of boats heading out for another day of fishing. I dressed and headed downstairs. I passed Harley's room, but it was empty. I found my father in the kitchen with a cup of coffee. He smiled as I walked in.

"Achilles. Did you sleep well?"

"I did." I poured a cup and joined him.

He always told me that money could buy many things, but it could never buy happiness, or life. I found it ironic that as much money as he had, the Parkinson's was taking its toll. There was only so much that could be done. I knew he was a fighter, because I got my fighting spirit from him.

"Harley is with your mother at the restaurant." My father grinned. "She is teaching him to make baklava."

"She better not let him drink." I snorted.

"Your mother explained everything to me about Harley. I am saddened to hear his parents are the way they are."

"I almost got into it with his father the night of the accident, Papa. I wanted to hurt him. I haven't felt that way since…" I swallowed hard. I would never forget the pain of that day. I'd wanted to die, but something kept me breathing.

"You have feelings for the boy." My father eyed me carefully.

"He's not a boy, Papa. He's older than me."

"Really? He looks so young." My father's brows creased. "He is still a boy to me."

"Yes, because you're ancient." I chuckled. I got a swat to my bicep and laughed even harder.

"Would you take me for a walk on the beach?" my father asked.

"Sure." I stood up and helped my father to stand.

We walked along the white sand beach, watching the water break along the rocks. It was beautiful, a lapis lazuli shade along the sand, and deep blue farther out. I loved coming home, it centered me in a way. I held my father's hand as we walked along, both of us just taking in the scenery before us.

"People should stop more often and enjoy what life has to offer," my father said, out of the blue. "I believe you are ready to move on, Achilles, and I believe Harley is the one for you."

"Well, if you could make him gay, that'd be great," I groused.

"I believe Harley does have feelings for you. I have seen the way he looks at you. Your mother has noticed as well."

"As much as I would like to believe that, I can't. I've been with them on their tours. Harley sleeps with women, Papa. He will never look at me in a romantic way."

"Why is it that the youth of today think they know better than us?" My father stopped and turned me to face him. "You have grieved for the loss of your love. It is time to open your heart again, Achilles. You have much to offer."

"You don't think I have deep feelings for Harley? You don't think it kills me to see him with women? Well, it does, Papa. It hurts like you wouldn't believe, but my job is to make sure he's not alone. My job is to make sure he doesn't hurt himself. The second I laid eyes on him, I knew, but it doesn't matter. My feelings are irrelevant."

"Maybe the gods will see fit to change Harley's mind."

I wrapped an arm around my father and started walking again.

"Maybe."

I watched in fascination as the large machine in front of me rolled out filo dough so thin I thought it would break. Another machine was working on chopping walnuts. And all the while, people were all over the kitchen making the meals for lunch that day. Calli was covered in flour, as was I, from making the dough. I was impressed. Everything was handmade in the kitchen, which was why the restaurant boasted of authentic Greek cuisine.

A few of the women in the kitchen had been eyeing me from the moment I walked in, but Achilles' mother had said something to them in Greek and they hadn't looked at me since. I heard Achilles' name mentioned quite a bit by the girls in the kitchen. Seemed he was very well liked by the staff — especially the women. One of them sidled up to me while Achilles' mother was at the stove.

"Achilles is home?" she asked innocently enough.

"Yes," I answered, taking in her appearance. She was definitely beautiful, with jet-black hair and piercing blue eyes. "Why?"

"We were hoping he would come. He always comes to help his mama out. You are his friend?"

"Um, yeah, sure."

"You tell him Jana ask after him?"

"Jana!" Calli barked. The girl next to me stood ramrod straight, her eyes cast downward. A slew of Greek flew past me and then Jana skittered across the room like a frightened mouse. Achilles' mother came to stand next to me, shaking her head.

"What is it? Is she an ex or something?" I asked.

"She wishes. They all do." Achilles' mother basically snorted. "Jana has had her eye on my Achilles since she was a little girl."

"He never dated her?" I glanced over my shoulder at Jana.

"No. Achilles has…different tastes." She glanced sideways at me with a coy smile. "What about you? What are your tastes?"

"Well, if you had asked me four or five months ago, I would have said Jana." I chuckled softly.

"And now?"

"Now? My tastes seem to have changed."

Calli shook her head firmly. "She is *not* my Achilles' lobster."

I snickered and Calli glanced at me.

"You know of what I speak?"

"I've seen the TV show, so yes — I know what you're talking about. Lobsters mate for life."

A ding went off in the kitchen somewhere and Calli strode across the floor to a large stove.

"Ah! The batch in the oven is done. Come taste!"

I stood by the counter as the baklava was cut into diamond shapes. Calli offered me one warm from the oven, honey dripping off the sides. I bit into it and almost moaned at the taste of nuts and sticky syrup. I could eat this stuff every day.

"Good?" Calli lifted a brow.

"Sooo good!" I mumbled around a mouthful.

Calli went to the other side of the kitchen and removed a large pan from the oven. She set it down on the counter and removed another dish from a nearby cabinet. After cutting whatever was in the big pan, she transferred it to the other one. I sniffed the air, my stomach grumbling.

"We will bring a pan of moussaka home for the men. Achilles and his father love it."

"What's in it?" I leaned over the pan and inhaled.

"Beef, eggplant, onions, tomato sauce, and a few other things. You like it?"

"I've never had it," I admitted.

"Now is your chance." She smiled, wrapping the pan in foil.

"I want to thank you for this, Calli. I love this place, it's so homey and it feels like family somehow."

"Everyone who works here worked here when my parents owned it. They've all grown up here. They stay because we treat them as family." Calli touched my cheek. "You are part of that family now, Harley."

I ducked my head as a blush rose to my cheeks. I was pulled into a hug, and then Calli kissed my forehead.

"You are ready to go?" she asked.

"Yes."

We passed Jana on the way out and she shoved something into my hand. She put a finger to her lips and walked away. I stuffed it in my pocket and kept walking. We passed through town on our way back and I was amazed to see how ancient it all looked. The island seemed to have been frozen in time. Here and there, you could tell it was evolving, but certain areas kept an authentic look.

"There are a lot of stone houses out here. It's so beautiful."

"We like to keep this island as close to the way it was as we can. We don't like outsiders coming in and trying to change it. They've offered to come and build huge hotels and we have always declined as a whole."

"Well, I love it."

"Achilles likes to come visit. We lived in New York for a little while, but this is home to Achilles."

Well, that explained the New York skyline on his bedroom wall. I wanted to know more about him; what made him happy, what he liked to do in his free time.

"What was he like growing up?" I heard myself asking.

"He was very curious. He needed to know how everything worked. I found him inside our TV one time."

"What?!" I laughed.

"Yes, the older ones, not like the flat screens of today. He'd taken the back off and had crawled inside. He took apart our car once, as well. I thought Krios was going to beat him, but Achilles remembered how to put it back together."

I laughed out loud. I couldn't even imagine Achilles as a child.

"Oh my God." I held my stomach.

"Do not tell him I told you, but he also did not like clothing. We found him naked all the time."

I spluttered and choked. Calli slid a sly look my way and grinned.

"I just can't even imagine him as a child. He's so…big."

"He is very tall like his father, and he ages well."

"How old is he?"

"He's twenty-seven."

My mouth fell open. Achilles was younger than me? Oh, I was going to *kill him* for treating me like a child! Calli must have caught on because in the next moment, she was holding my hand.

"He has always been the responsible kind, Harley. Do not be angry with him for his behavior. I am sure whatever he has done, he has done for you."

Yeah, I caught on to that last night when he told his parents I was just his job. My heart ached again just remembering it. I felt my pocket, the note for Jana was still there, and I didn't know if I wanted to give it to Achilles or not. What if it was a love letter or something? What if Achilles hooked up while we were here? Fuck, I couldn't keep it from him. What if he truly had feelings for this girl?

"Ah, we are home," Calli announced as we headed up the driveway. "Maybe tonight you can take a walk on the beach? It is beautiful at night."

"Maybe." I nodded.

As we entered the house, Achilles walked into the foyer and helped his mother with the pan of moussaka. He sniffed it with a grin. Right then, I could see the child in Achilles. I threw him a look which said *we'll talk later*, and his brows creased in confusion. I smiled wickedly and entered the kitchen. Achilles' father was seated at the table and a chessboard was set up.

"Thank God. I thought I would lose to my son again." Krios lightly laughed. "Did you enjoy your day, Harley?"

"I really did!" I enthused. "It was really cool to see how stuff is made. I don't cook much." Achilles snorted and I shot him a look.

"Well, shall we eat?" Calli quickly interrupted.

As we sat around the table talking and laughing over the food, I felt as if I'd been missing out my entire life on what it was like to be part of a family. It made me miss Holden even more. I'd never had this with my own parents, and I was almost jealous that Achilles had such a close relationship with his.

"Harley, are you all right?" Achilles asked in a hushed tone.

"Yes, I'm just tired, I guess. Would you all mind if I headed upstairs?"

"By all means." Calli stood with me and pulled me into a hug. "I had a wonderful time with you today, Harley."

"Thank you. Me too."

I had to get out of there. I excused myself and practically ran up the stairs. Once I got to my room, I shut the door and walked out onto my balcony. It overlooked the ocean, and I stared up into the night sky with a half moon that seemed to be closer than normal. I took deep breaths, fighting back the emotion just under the surface. I missed Holden so much.

"Can you see me, Holden?" I whispered to the night sky. "I miss you."

There was a knock on my door and I walked across the room to answer it. Achilles stood with a plate of baklava and a smile.

"Hey, I thought you might like this in your room."

"Thank you."

"Are you okay?" He tilted his head, searching my eyes.

"I'm just," I sighed, walking back out onto the balcony. "I wish I had what you have."

"You can," Achilles said from behind me.

I turned to look at him. "How would that happen, Achilles? My parents don't even know I'm alive. I might as well not even exist."

"Don't you ever say that again!" Achilles shouted at me. He seemed to be surprised at his own outburst, and took a deep breath. "I'm sorry, I didn't mean to yell at you."

"I didn't know you could." I gave him a lopsided grin.

"Funny." Achilles frowned.

I felt my pocket and removed the slip of paper, handing it to him. He looked it over and his eyes met mine with a look of confusion.

"What's this?"

"A message from Jana, I believe."

Achilles ran a hand through his hair and let out what sounded like an irritated sigh. He opened the note and read it. I tried to get a peek, but I didn't read Greek.

"What's it say?" I asked.

"She wants me to meet her tonight by the temple."

"Oh," I said, a bit dejected.

"Not going to happen." Achilles ripped up the note and stuffed it in his pocket. "How about you and I take a walk instead?"

"Are you sure? She was pretty and she seems to want you."

"Why don't you meet her then?" Achilles snapped.

"Whoa." I took a step back.

"Fuck! I'm sorry. I need to go."

I stood there in stunned silence as Achilles stalked out of my room, slamming the door behind him. Well, fuck me running. What the fuck was that all about? I stood there for what seemed like an hour trying to process what had just happened. I didn't think I'd done anything wrong. Anger began to boil in my gut and I stalked across the room, flinging the door open and walking down the hall to

Achilles' room. I could hear music playing behind the door and I cracked it a bit, peeking in.

Achilles was shirtless, doing push-ups. My eyes roamed along his strong back, the way his muscles tensed when he dipped to the floor. The music sounded familiar, like I'd heard it in a movie somewhere. I stepped into the room and slammed the door shut. Achilles stopped mid push-up and looked up.

"What the fuck was that?" I crossed my arms over my chest. "And what is this song?"

"It's Moby. 'Find my baby'. Why?"

"Answer the first question."

Achilles stood up and wiped his forearm across his temple. "I said I was sorry, okay?"

"Did I do something wrong?"

"No. It's just me, okay?" Achilles paced the room. "I'm going for a swim."

"Are you nuts? What's the water temperature?"

"I don't know, sixties?" Achilles grabbed his shoes and walked past me.

"Are you trying to get sick?" I followed him out.

"I'll be fine. I do it all the time." Achilles grabbed a towel out of the linen closet and I almost had to run to keep up with his fast pace.

We headed down the path to the beach and Achilles ran for the water, almost tripping trying to get his sweats off. I was really hoping he was naked under them, but no such luck. He was wearing boxers. Achilles hit the water and went under. I stood on shore, holding a towel for when he came back out.

The moon's rays lit up the water and my mouth fell open at the beauty before me. Achilles had surfaced, water dripping down his massive chest. He shook his hair out and I swallowed the lump in my throat. In all my life, I'd never seen anything as breathtaking as Achilles Castellanos. He slowly walked out of the water and my heart beat in time with his gait. Achilles stood in front of me, droplets of water running between his pectorals. I wanted to touch him, feel his heart beat under my palm.

"Achilles," I whispered.

I placed my hand on his chest and closed my eyes. Life beat there, the thumping of Achilles' heart filled my senses. I'd never wanted someone so much in my life. Achilles' hand came over the top of mine and I opened my eyes to find him watching me intently. His fingers threaded with mine and my heart skipped a beat. I wanted to see in his eyes what I felt just then, an innate need to kiss him, hold him. I wanted him to want me the way I wanted him. Achilles' hand hovered by my face and finally rested on my cheek. I leaned into it, a soft sigh escaping me as Achilles caressed my cheek with his thumb.

"You are worth so much more than you think, Harley," Achilles murmured. "You are truly a blessing in this world, and anyone who doesn't see that doesn't deserve to be in your life."

"Why don't they love me?" I glanced up at him and was shocked to see Achilles' eyes. They were filled with so much sadness, it broke my heart.

"Because they don't see you," Achilles choked out.

He was shaking, but I didn't know if that was from the cold or the conversation. I wrapped the towel around him and took his hand. "Come on, let's get you inside and warmed up."

I stood on the veranda as Achilles showered. I looked up into the night sky and for the hundredth time, wondered if Holden was up there watching me. Tomorrow was another day, and I hoped Achilles and I would spend it together doing something fun. After tonight, I needed some fun. I went back to my room and settled in under the covers. Achilles poked his head in and I sat up a bit.

"Goodnight, Harley," he said quietly.

"Achilles?"

"Yes?"

"Thank you for what you said tonight."

"It's the truth, Harley."

Achilles closed the door and I sat there thinking about what had transpired on the beach. Was I just seeing what I wanted to see? Or did I really see what I wanted in Achilles' eyes? I rolled to my side on a soft sigh and closed my eyes.

Chapter 11

Achilles

I woke up at five in the morning and went for a run on the beach. I needed to clear my head. I'd almost lost it completely on Harley last night. Not only did I yell at him, but I was also seconds from kissing him on the beach. The hurt in his voice when he asked why his parents didn't love him, it struck me so hard I almost couldn't breathe. I ran to the docks and stopped, watching the men getting ready to go out for the day, all of them huddled around old oil barrels, warming their hands over the flames that licked upwards. I stood on the seasoned wood, looking out over the water. I reached into my pocket and pulled out the white envelope I had long ago set between two books.

I opened it carefully and began to read the last words of the man I had loved so long ago.

Achilles,

Even now, I feel like a coward as I write this. Afraid someone will wonder why I would leave a letter to my partner. You deserved so much better than I gave you. I should have shouted it from the rooftops that you were mine. I should have told you every day that I loved you. I should have done a lot of things. And if you're reading this letter, it's because I died without telling you how much you meant to me. I do love you, I loved you from the moment I saw you and I'm so sorry I didn't tell you. I hope that one day you can find it in your heart to forgive me. You deserve someone who will love you openly. Honestly. Of all the things I wish for, I wish for you to find love again. I will hold you close to my heart forevermore, Achilles.

All my love,

Brian.

I wiped at my eyes and lifted my head to see the sun rising on the horizon. Life went on, and I had to go on with it. I had another chance at love with Harley, but he needed to face his grief. I felt it last night. My parents were right; Harley did harbor feelings for me. I stepped up to the barrel and took one last look at the letter.

"Bye, Brian," I whispered, dropping it in the flames.

I ran back toward the house, pushing my limits. I needed to let everything go. I needed to cleanse my soul. I kept running all the way to Apollo's temple. I stopped and inhaled sharply. My lungs were on fire and I sat down on the edge of the cliff, watching the water roll in and out, letting my breaths move with it. I couldn't deny my feelings anymore. Somewhere along the way, I had fallen for Harley Payne. Silly, sarcastic, naked-running--through-the-streets, Harley Payne. The moment I met him, I knew he was special. I smiled and tipped my face to the sun.

"Hey."

I almost fell off the cliff from the shock and glanced over my shoulder to see Harley toeing the dirt.

"Hi." I stood up and walked over to him. "What are you doing here?"

"Um, your mom said you sometimes run up here." Harley glanced over at the temple. "It really is beautiful."

"Why don't I take you to see the sights today?"

"Really?" Harley ducked his head with a grin. "You wouldn't mind?"

"Nope." I shook my head. "But I do need to shower first."

"Good, because I was about to comment on your stench."

I gave him a wicked grin and Harley sprinted off, laughing as he did. I chased him down the beach. The little shit was fast. The sound of his laughter was like a siren's song. His hair floated with the wind, almost like a halo around his head, and his eyes were bright with mirth. I caught him near the stairs and grabbed him, holding him firmly to my chest. Harley wrapped his arms around my neck and looked up with a devilish grin.

"For someone so young, you sure are slow."

"Ah," I nodded. "You finally figured out how old I am."

"Yes and it pisses me off to no end that you act older. And bossier."

I put him down on the ground and tucked a piece of wild hair behind his ear. "I know when your birthday is."

"You do?" Harley cocked his head to the side.

"Yes. Christmas Eve. You were born at eleven fifty nine p.m."

"Jinx told you," Harley whined.

"No. Paul did." That seemed to shock him and I grinned. "I did go see Paul while we were in Los Angeles."

"So did I. He didn't mention that you had, though."

"Probably slipped his mind." I shrugged. "Let's eat and get ready to go."

~*~

After eating with my parents, I drove Harley to the other side of the island to see the monastery first. We played car games on the way and Harley cracked me up with his "Oh, nope, another Greek license plate."

Once we arrived, Harley grew serious as we entered the grounds of the convent. Potted rose bushes and other flowers lined both sides of the path as we walked toward the church itself. The scents of drying herbs and the sounds of swallows nesting filled the air. Once inside, Harley stood in awe, as did I, at the scene before us. Large chandeliers hung from the ceiling and religious icons were carved into the stone painted in vivid colors.

"Wow," Harley gasped. "I've never seen anything like it," he whispered.

"I love coming here," I replied in the same tone. "I always have a sense of peace."

We walked along outside, Harley enchanted by the grounds and the carvings. When we finally got back in the car, I could tell he was excited to see more. He watched eagerly out the window as we drove.

"No wonder everyone out here has a tiny car. You can only fit one on the road."

"Well, you also see a lot of people riding bikes."

"Which temple is that?" Harley pointed out the window.

"Temple of Zeus."

"Look at all the trees. What are they?"

"Pistachio. This island has figs, as well as olives and almonds."

Harley was so excited; he was bouncing in his seat. I loved seeing him like that. So full of life. We parked and walked up to the temple. A few other tourists were making the rounds and snapping pictures. Harley stood in front of the large columns and whistled.

"What it must have been like to be alive back then," he contemplated.

"I've often wondered what it would have been like. Living here, seeing the temples, walking the same earth they did."

"You must love coming here. I'd want to come all the time."

"Well, we have another temple to visit if you're up for it."

"Lead the way."

The sun was setting as we parked near the temple of Apollo. My parents' house was just over the ridge from it, so I decided to hit it last. Harley would have to see it at night.

"It's a big fishing place, huh?" Harley stood on the cliff, watching the fishing ships below.

"Yes, they fish sponge mostly."

"Sponge?"

"Yes, slimy suckers."

"Isn't there a temple of Apollo in Italy?"

"Yes. There are quite a few. I think you are speaking of the one in Pompeii."

"You sounded so Greek just now," Harley snickered.

"What is the origin of Payne?"

"English or French." Harley shrugged. "Jinx swears it's French, I think he just wants to share that with me."

"You miss him." I tilted my head, watching Harley.

"Yeah. I do, but I get it. When you find someone who makes you whole, you want to spend all your time with them."

"Come on, let's get closer."

We spent an hour taking pictures in front of the temple. Harley posed in front of the columns and I couldn't help but admire him through the lens.

I took him down the path and we walked along the water's edge. Boats bobbed up and down on the water and the moon hung in the sky like a huge beacon, beckoning the fishermen to shore. I'd always loved it out here; the sounds, the smells, the sights. Greece was always home to me. Lights lit the entire shore, and the temple of Apollo was bathed in it. I turned Harley around to face it and a gasp escaped him.

"Wow! That is so beautiful!"

"I never get tired of seeing it. I always used to come out here at night and just sit, wondering what it was like to be alive back then, to be a Trojan warrior."

"Is that why they named you Achilles?" Harley climbed up one of the rocks along the shore and sat down.

"I was a big baby and I had a head full of hair when I was born. My mother wanted to name me after a great warrior. So here I am."

"I was named after a motorcycle." Harley chuckled. "Not that I mind. If I ever have a kid, I'll give it an awesome name like Hawk or something."

"Hawk?" I snickered.

"Sure, why not? Poor Paul was the only guy who had a normal name in school. Rebel got his because he was constantly crawling out of his crib and he came early."

"Yeah? What about Ransom?"

"His mom loved the name, so she gave it to him."

I sat down next to Harley and propped my arms over my knees. "So you want kids then?"

"Yes. I want at least two, that way they have each other. I'm going to do right by my kids."

"What will their mother look like?" I glanced off to the sea when I asked that because I really didn't want to know. I wanted Harley for myself and God help me, I knew I shouldn't. He was my charge and I needed to focus on that.

"Maybe I'll adopt, who knows? I can't see myself in a relationship with a woman long term."

"Why not?"

"Um, we should get back, right?" Harley stood up and began crawling down the rocks.

"Harley, wait." I caught up to him in the sand and took his hand. He looked down at our hands and then back up at me.

"What?" he asked.

"Why didn't you answer me?"

"It's not a big deal, okay? Just let it go."

"I want to know," I pressed.

"Why? I'm just your job, right? It's not like you give a fuck about my life."

My mouth hung open and Harley began walking back toward the villa. My brain kicked in, propelling me forward in the sand. I caught up to him by the stairs heading up to the house.

"Whoa, wait a sec." I took his hand. "What the hell was that?"

"I heard you! You basically told your parents I'm just a job to you! That's fine, it's not like I'm not used to being treated like a job. I'm a pain in the ass, a mistake —"

"What the hell, Harley?! Is that what you really think of me? Jesus, when you crashed the bike, I thought I was going to lose my fucking mind! I thought you'd fly over that cliff and then you'd be gone. When you were sick, I wanted to take your pain away, I would have done anything to take that from you. Don't you get it?" I took his face in my hands. "I *see* you! Do you understand me? I've always *seen* you!"

Harley blinked and his eyes filled with tears. I leaned in, a hair's breadth from his lips. Our eyes met and his lips parted. That was enough for me. I caught his lips with mine, savoring the taste of him slowly. My hand went to his nape and I pulled him up into the kiss. Harley invited me in, his tongue sliding erotically against mine. I couldn't catch my breath, couldn't feel anything but Harley's warmth. His body melded to mine as the kiss deepened. I tried to convey everything I was feeling in that moment, so Harley would understand he wasn't alone. He'd never be alone again. His arms wrapped around my neck and he gave himself to me freely. I broke from the kiss slowly, leaving soft kisses on his lips. I thumbed a tear from his cheek and palmed his face.

"Do you hear me, Harley Payne?" I whispered. "I see you."

Harley nodded and then he was on me, his lips crashing hot and hard into mine. I grabbed him around his waist and hoisted him up, holding him close to me as we kissed. I nipped at his lips, loving the taste of his flesh on mine. My whole body erupted in chaos as Harley licked at the inside of my mouth, his hands threading into my hair, his soft mewls fueling my desire for him.

We broke from the kiss, gasping for air. Harley's awestruck eyes met mine and a look of confusion crossed his features. I caressed his cheek, searching his eyes.

"What?" I asked, curious.

"This feels like déjà vu." Harley's brows creased in concentration. "I've kissed you before."

"Yes." I nodded slowly.

"You kissed me back." Harley searched my features. "Why?"

"Because I wanted to. I've wanted to kiss you for a long time, Harley."

"You have?" Harley asked in astonishment. "But you never said anything."

"I thought you were straight. I didn't want to get hurt falling for a straight guy."

"I thought you were straight, too." Harley chuckled quietly. He sobered and eyed me. "You're falling for me?"

"I was falling for you the second you ran down the street in your boxers."

Harley grinned and touched my face. "I didn't know. I thought all this time you were just saddled with me and hated every second of it."

"I've loved every second I've spent with you, Harley Payne. You're not just a job to me. You never were."

"I've been falling for you from the minute you stepped foot in the room, I just didn't know it. Then you would be on my ass night and day —"

I snickered and Harley narrowed his eyes at me.

"You didn't want me to be with women?"

"No. I didn't. I still don't. I want you with me, Harley."

"Really? Why?"

"Because I love that you would do anything for your friends. I love that you came here with me and spent the day with my mother. I love that when you sing, you open yourself up fully. And I love that even after the way you've been treated, you still bring love to others. Look, I know you're probably not ready for me, but when you are, I'll be right here. Waiting."

My mom's voice carried along the wind and I looked up toward the house. She was waving at us from the veranda. I took Harley's hand and he looked down, threading his fingers into mine.

"Come on." Harley smiled up at me. "I think it's dinner time."

Achilles and I ascended the steps to the house, holding hands. His warmth and words settled into me, heating me from the inside. Achilles had wanted me all this time? I kept sneaking looks at him as we took the stairs. Our eyes would meet and he would give me a reassuring smile. I let go of his hand as we reached the back door and Achilles stopped me.

"My parents know I'm gay," he explained.

"Gay, gay?"

"Yep. Just gay. That's why meeting Jana would have been a waste of her time. I didn't find her attractive back then, and I sure don't now."

"Wow. I didn't know. I assumed you were straight."

"Seems there's a lot of assumptions going on tonight." Achilles narrowed his eyes at me.

I couldn't stop staring at his mouth or his lips. Just remembering the kiss on the beach had me sweating. I wanted this man like no other. Achilles leaned into me and smiled.

"What are you thinking?" he asked.

Calli poked her head out the door. "Achilles, Harley! There you are. Come in for supper!"

I waited until she'd gone back in and arched a brow at Achilles, giving him my best seductive grin. "Wouldn't you like to know?"

I swear to God, he growled at me and my skin rippled up my back. Fuck, that was sexy! I chuckled instead and entered the house. Calli had made quite the spread and I sat down at the table right next to Achilles' father.

"Did you have a fun day, Harley?" Krios asked.

"I really did." I locked onto Achilles' eyes. A slow smile spread across my features as Achilles' face turned slightly pink. I told them all about our trip into town as I ate. Calli had made a wonderful salad with huge black and green olives. We passed the bowls around the table, Achilles laughing as he told them all about my modeling poses in front of the temples. I watched them all intently; the way they laughed, the way Calli's eyes crinkled in the corners, Krios wiping at his eyes. Calli would place her hand on mine when she broke into laughter, and then kiss my head. I knew I was smiling and I couldn't stop. This was what I'd wanted. A family.

"Harley? I wonder if you would play a song for me?" Krios asked.

"I would love to." Achilles snickered and I eyeballed him over the table. "I *can* sing something soft ya know."

"Let us go to the other room." Calli stood. "Achilles, can you start a fire?"

"Yes, Mama."

I ran upstairs to get my guitar. I was nervous to play in front of Achilles' parents. What if they didn't like it? I came back down to find them sitting on the couch in the living room. A fire was flickering in the fireplace. I sat down across from them and placed my guitar in my lap.

"My brother always loved this song, so I'll play it."

I closed my eyes, exhaled and strummed the guitar strings. My brother cherished his Queensryche CD and one song, "Silent Lucidity." I knew the lyrics backwards and forwards from him listening to it on repeat. I lifted my head as I sang and found them all watching me intently. Achilles was watching me in wonder, and Calli had a tear in her eye. Whenever I sang the song, it always reminded me of Holden, as if somehow, he knew one day he would be gone and he would always be watching out for me.

Now I had Achilles watching out for me. I wouldn't have that part any other way. I thumbed the last of the strings and closed my eyes. Clapping erupted and I stood up, taking a slight bow.

"My God, Harley! You have a beautiful voice!" Calli hugged me.

"The song was beautiful, Harley. I didn't know it, but you sang it wonderfully." Krios stood and held me to him. "Thank you so much."

"You're welcome." I hugged him back.

"I will retire now." Krios kissed Calli's cheek and hugged Achilles.

"I'll walk you up, Papa." Achilles took his father by the elbow.

I watched them ascend the steps and then placed my guitar up against the couch. Calli sat down and regarded me thoughtfully.

"You like my son," she blurted out.

"I didn't know…" I began to babble.

"No, most don't. I don't spread my son's sexuality; it's not my place and it's no one's business. But when you came into his life, I saw a light shine in Achilles I hadn't seen in quite a long time. We almost lost him. When we were called to Germany, we didn't think he would ever awaken from his coma. I sat by my son's bed day in and day out just waiting for that one twitch, that one eyelash flutter. The doctors told us he wouldn't awaken again, but I knew." Calli wiped her eyes and glanced off to the side. "My son is a fighter, and when he finally woke, he cried.

He cried for all the men he couldn't save, and for the one he loved and lost."

I started at that. Achilles had been in love?

"When he is ready, he will tell you." Calli took my hands. "I see a light in you, Harley. It is so bright, it calls out. Children, no matter how they come into our lives, are never a mistake. Each life is a miracle, Harley. I believe you were meant to be here, and I find my life enriched just by knowing you."

I nodded because I knew if I said anything, I would cry. I swore I'd never cry. Calli took me into her embrace and I held her hard.

"You are so very special, Harley Payne," she whispered, "Don't ever think less. Mourn for the one you lost and let him go. The best way to honor him is to live."

Calli placed a kiss on my cheek and stood. "I'll go now. Please remember what I have said, Harley. You are already part of this family."

I stood as she walked toward the stairs. I'd barely known these people for two days and they welcomed me into their hearts and home. I stared into the fire and then closed my eyes, taking deep breaths.

"It's okay to cry, Harley."

I turned to find Achilles behind me. He walked over to me slowly, his hands stuffed in his pockets.

"It's all right to be angry."

"Who am I angry at?" I asked.

Achilles stood in front of me and took my hands. "When you're ready, you'll know. I'm not going to push, but you need to grieve for your loss."

"I already did that." I shook my head.

"Did you?" Achilles lifted my face with his fingers. "I want you, Harley Payne. All of you. When you're ready for that, let me know."

Achilles kissed my lips gently and walked away. I sat down on the floor and picked up my guitar, playing the same song again. I knew what I wanted.

Achilles Castellanos.

~*~

We were all at the restaurant the next day, helping Calli in the kitchen. Achilles was wooing the women in the dining room as he played the role of waiter. From the moment we walked in, I think I heard a collective swoon from every female customer. I couldn't blame them. Achilles was, as I'd said, an Adonis. Jana threw me some nasty looks whenever Achilles would bend down and whisper in my ear. She actually dragged me aside within the first two minutes to ask if I'd given Achilles the note. I assured her I had and she walked off mumbling something under her breath. I really needed to learn Greek.

"Come, Harley! We are toasting to Achilles being home!" Calli squealed.

I entered the dining room and a waitress handed me a shot glass. Achilles eyed me from across the room and I smiled wickedly as I sniffed the alcohol. I didn't plan on drinking any more than what I had in my hand. I wasn't going to run around the island naked and disappoint Achilles' parents. Achilles' mom made the toast and then we all took our shots. I coughed and choked as the alcohol burned down the back of my throat. Calli slapped my back and I laughed.

It seemed as if everyone in the place knew Achilles. They all hugged him, patted his shoulders and kissed his cheeks. I watched closely as Jana approached him. He bent down to her level to hear what she was saying and he shook his head, leading her off to one of the corners. I knew I shouldn't be jealous, but I was. Achilles held Jana's hand, and I could see his lips moving. Jana shot a glance at me and then looked up at Achilles, nodding slowly. Calli came to stand next to me and we both watched Achilles.

"I believe he is telling her the truth," Calli commented.

Achilles hugged Jana and she gave him a warm smile as she went back to the kitchen. He righted himself and then turned to see Calli and me watching him. He crossed the room and took my hand.

"Um, what was all that?" I asked.

"Just letting Jana know where my heart lies. She's okay. She's actually happy it wasn't another girl," Achilles snickered.

"Achilles, why don't you take Harley over to the Lambros farm? I am sure they need help."

"Are you sure? I can stay and help here," Achilles answered.

"No. I will be fine. I can have Jana drive me home."

"Okay." Achilles kissed her cheeks and turned to me. "Ready to go have fun?"

"Um. Sure?"

Achilles laughed and pulled me along.

~*~

Ten minutes later, we were pulling up to a beautiful villa covered in climbing vines. Achilles jumped out of the car and came around to my side. He helped me out and we walked toward the front door. It opened suddenly and a young man walked out. Achilles started and then a grin covered his face.

"Phoinix!" he shouted. "What are you doing here?"

"I am on vacation." Phoinix's eyes landed on me and he jerked his chin to Achilles. "Who is this?"

"Look closely, my friend." Achilles laughed.

Phoinix came closer and a huge grin split his face. "Oh my God! It's Harley Payne!"

I was pulled into a hug and squashed within an inch of my life. I hugged him back and he pulled away, still holding my shoulders.

"You rock! I love the Skull Blasters!" he enthused.

"Thank you," I answered with a grin.

"What brings you to Greece?" Phoinix asked.

"This guy." I jerked a thumb to Achilles. "His mom sent us over to help with something?"

"Cool. I was just coming out to grab the truck. You can ride with me." Phoinix grabbed Achilles' hand. "I missed you."

I followed behind them as they walked over to an older pickup truck, the two of them chatting away like they'd known each other forever.

"Um, how long have you known each other?" I asked.

"I met Achilles when he was twelve or so. I was two years behind him. He went off to the Army and then I joined the Hellenic Army when I was old enough," Phoinix explained.

We all jumped in the truck and Phoinix fired it up, rounding the corner and taking us behind the villa. My eyes widened as I took in the amount of land in front of us.

"Wow, are those all pistachio trees?" I asked.

"Oh no, there are fig, almond, and two kinds of olive out here, as well as pistachio. We also have lamb that we use for cheese, clothing, and other foods."

"Meaning lamb shank." Achilles licked his lips with a wicked grin.

"So, what are we helping with?" I asked curiously.

"You'll see." Achilles smiled.

I was sitting on the floor twenty minutes later with a huge pile of black olives between my legs. Achilles had his own and was picking between them, throwing out molded or bruised ones into a bowl. I picked one up and inspected it.

"This one's good, right?" I showed Achilles.

"Yes. If you see white on them, or indentations that are too deep, drop them in that bowl. Good ones go into this one." Achilles pulled the bowl between us.

"Do you do this a lot?" I asked, inspecting another one.

"Whenever I come home. Our restaurant uses everything this farm makes, be it nuts, olives or lamb."

Phoinix walked in with a huge basket full of green olives and plopped down on the floor with them.

"Yes, Achilles' family has kept mine in the black for years. My parents truly appreciate their business." Phoinix eyed me. "How did Achilles end up with you?"

"This is my job now, Phoinix. I'm a bodyguard," Achilles replied.

"Yeah? Is it lucrative?" Phoinix wiggled his brows.

"I would say yes. Maybe when you get out, you should look up my boss. I'll give you a glowing recommendation."

We spent hours sifting through olives, something I didn't think I'd ever be doing — but like coloring, it was extremely relaxing. Phoinix regaled me with tales of a young Achilles while we sorted. I couldn't believe how much fun I was having. Achilles was laughing and smiling, and it was perfect. Once we finished that batch, Achilles and I went for a walk among the many trees. He stopped at one and pulled a branch down.

"What's that one?" I asked.

"Fig tree. They are in season in September. Have you ever had a fig?"

"I'm sure I've had a fig bar at some point. I like them." Achilles began walking again and I stood my ground. "Who were you in love with, Achilles?"

He stopped and hung his head. I heard a soft curse, and then he turned to face me.

"My mom?"

I nodded.

"Come here." Achilles motioned to the tree and he sat down, holding his hand out to me. I took a seat next to him and he wrapped an arm around my shoulder. I leaned into him, laying my head against his shoulder.

"I met Brian when I was in sniper school. Eventually, he became my spotter. We spent a lot of hours together and that led to us goofing off sometimes, and one night, he kissed me."

Achilles sighed and stared up at the sky.

"Neither one of us was out, but I think I was a little more lax than he was. I could never hold his hand, kiss him, or be near him in public off the job, and that took a toll on us. I wanted more and he couldn't give it to me. That night, the night we were ambushed, I tried to shield him with my own body, but I still failed. One of the bullets went through me and hit him in the neck. I tried everything to keep him alive, and even approaching his own death, staring right at me, he couldn't say the words."

I took Achilles' hand and held it. It must have hurt him to the core and I didn't know how to make it better.

"I'm so sorry," I whispered inadequately.

"I stayed there with him, still hoping against hope that somehow, someway, they could bring him back. My arms burned and I couldn't breathe, but I still got up, I still held that rifle in my hand and killed as many of them as I could before the chopper came in and leveled everything. It wasn't until I woke up in the hospital months later that I was handed Brian's letter. He said he loved me, but it was a little late in coming."

"At least you knew he loved you, right? That has to mean something."

"It would have made all the difference in the world if I could have heard it, Harley. My road to recovery was riddled with anger and doubt and all the while, my mother pushed me to be better. I owe her a lot for coming through this with my head still intact."

I palmed his cheek and stared into his eyes. Achilles leaned in and I met him halfway. Our lips touched softly and an electric current ran down the length of me. His hand went to my cheek, and then to my nape as his mouth opened to mine. I whimpered as he pulled me into him, our tongues sliding and curling around each other. Achilles broke from the kiss and rubbed his nose on mine.

"We better go before we get carried away," he panted.

I nodded, reluctantly, and Achilles stood, holding a hand out to me. I placed my hand in his and he lifted me from the ground. We stood there just staring at each other for the longest time.

"Have you ever been with a guy, Harley?"

I blinked and my mouth fell open in surprise.

"Is that a no?" Achilles searched my eyes.

"I actually have," I admitted. "I was the pitcher, as Gareth says."

"Okay, good. I'm a catcher."

Achilles began walking and I froze up, almost tripping in surprise. "I'm sorry, could you repeat that?"

Achilles stopped walking and turned with a smile on his face. He walked back to me and looked deeply into my eyes.

"I'm in control of everything around me, Harley. I like feeling out of control in the bedroom. Are you any good?"

"What kind of question is that?" I narrowed my eyes at him.

"Guess we'll have to find out." Achilles turned on his heel and began walking again.

"Achilles-whatever-your-middle-name is-Castellanos! You do not get to say something like that and walk away from me!"

Achilles' laughter carried on the wind and I ran to catch up. Phoinix was seated on the back porch waiting for us when we got back.

"My father thanks you for all your help today. Your mother called, she is at home now."

"Thanks, Phoinix. We'll head out now. Have fun while you're on vacation."

"You as well. It was nice to meet you, Harley Payne. I hope before you leave you can sign something for me?"

"Of course!" I assured him.

"Okay! Wait right there!" Phoinix almost squealed. I turned to Achilles. "He really is excited."

"When they told me who I was going to work for, I reacted about the same way." Achilles shrugged.

"Really?"

"No." Achilles grinned and I swatted his arm.

Phoinix came back out with a pen and two of our albums and a huge poster. I signed all three and handed him back the pen.

"Maybe when you come visit America, you can get the rest of the guys to sign it."

"I would love that! Thank you both for coming today and helping. I hope to come visit soon."

"Why don't we go out tonight?" Achilles asked.

"Really?" Phoinix glanced over at me.

"Sure, why not?" I agreed. "Where?"

"There is a karaoke bar here. We could head over after dinner?" Achilles asked.

"Sounds perfect!" Phoinix practically bounced on his toes. "I will come by."

"See you tonight, Phoinix." I shook his hand.

I made good on my promise to play video games with Titus. Harley was seated on the couch across from us as Titus and I fought to the death in "Tekken." We'd had dinner already and I'd let my parents know I was going to take Harley out and meet up with Phoinix. Titus landed a roundhouse kick to my face and I stared at him in surprise.

"You've been practicing!" I accused.

Titus chuckled and Harley broke out in laughter. We'd been playing for almost an hour, and in that time, I'd won two games. I narrowed my eyes at Titus and he feigned a look of innocence.

"I do not know what you are talking about." He tried to look hurt.

"Who helped you, huh?" I glared at him.

"That would be me," Phoinix said from behind us.

I turned on the couch and pointed a finger at him. "Not fair!"

"I am done for tonight anyway." Titus stood up and handed the controller to Harley.

"We're going out," I said, standing and turning the game off. I hugged Titus and he kissed my cheek.

"Have fun tonight!" Titus mussed Harley's hair on his way out.

I let my parents know we were leaving and then jumped into the car with Harley and Phoinix. We hit the road and Harley turned in the front seat to look back at Phoinix.

"You play a lot of video games?" he asked.

"When I am on vacation, I like doing nothing. It's relaxing." Phoinix grinned.

"I like to color," Harley admitted.

"With crayons?" Phoinix asked.

"Yes," I answered before Harley could. "Believe me, it really is stress relieving."

We pulled up to the club and I parked off to the side. The parking lot was already crammed with compact cars and all sorts of bikes. Harley jumped out of the car and looked up at the blinking neon sign. I stood next to him as a guitar blinked on and off in blue and white.

"Cool." Harley tilted his head. "I need one of those."

"Uh huh." I laughed, pulling him inside by his bicep.

Phoinix trailed behind us as we headed to the bar. The bar was filled with people, mostly drunks trying to sing karaoke. I winced as a man tried to hit a high note and the mic squealed in response.

"Ow." Harley covered his ears.

"What do you want to drink?" I practically shouted.

"You mean I can?" Harley responded in the same fashion.

"I'll watch out for you," I assured him.

"Ouzo!" Harley laughed.

"He's crazy." Phoenix pointed at Harley.

"You have no idea," I sighed.

An hour later, I was seated in the front row as Phoinix and Harley sang karaoke for the drunken clientele. They had gone through some Seventies songs and then had gotten back onstage for the Eighties. I hadn't stopped laughing since they sang the first one. Harley was pointing at the monitor and Phoinix was grinning as they cued up another song.

"The Tubes!" Harley shouted into the microphone.

"She's a beautyyyy!" Phoinix slurred.

I leaned back in the chair and crossed my arms as Harley bounced around on stage singing. He was changing the she's to he's and pointing to me as he did. I covered my face with my hands and exhaled slowly. If there was one thing I loved about my job, it was the crazy guy running across the stage right now, singing perfectly.

Oh, ouzo was a bitch.

Phoinix was bumping into Harley and both of them were cracking up. I smiled and then laughed. I couldn't help it. The two of them were so comical, the whole place was busting up. Amazingly, Harley sounded good even drunk. The song ended and Harley almost tripped and face planted coming off the stage. I was at his side in a split second and he looked up at me with a huge smile.

"He's one in a million guysssss!"

"Oh, I think we're done here." I grabbed Phoinix by his bicep and began walking.

"Wait a minute!" Phoinix grabbed a glass off the table as we walked by, swigging down the remaining liquid. "Okay, now we can go."

Harley snorted in laughter and I couldn't stop the grin forming on my lips. These two were going to be a handful. I got Phoinix in the car and then settled Harley in the passenger seat.

"How did I sound, Achilles?" Phoinix asked, leaning on the back of our seats.

"I don't know if I should answer that."

"You were good!" Harley clapped his hands.

"You are just saying that." Phoinix rolled down the window and stuck his head out.

"Don't puke on the car!" I pulled over and put the car in park. Phoinix was leaning out the window as I opened the door and he came with it. I untangled him and helped him to stand.

"I'm not going to puke. I just needed air." Phoinix grinned up at me. "Seems you found the one for you?"

I glanced over at Harley, who was passed out in the front seat. I shook my head with a smile.

"What makes you say that?" I asked.

"I see the way he looks at you." Phoinix closed his eyes. "I would like that someday."

"You'll have it."

"Maybe."

I helped him back in the car and drove him home, getting out of the car to walk him up to the door. Phoinix's father opened the door and a wry smile lifted his lips.

"Singing?"

"Yes."

"Thank you for bringing him home, Achilles. Have a good night."

"You as well!"

I drove home and parked the car in the garage. I looked over to see Harley completely passed out. I chuckled and got out, going around to his side. Harley was not small, by any means. He was six foot and weighed at least one hundred and seventy pounds. I moved him carefully and picked him up in my arms. He sighed and his head lolled into my shoulder. I stared at him. Even in sleep, he was perfection. His lips were so damned soft. I licked my lips just looking at them.

I carried Harley upstairs and placed him in bed gently. He rolled and mumbled something in his sleep, and I leaned over to hear him better.

"Harley?" I whispered.

"You make things better," Harley mumbled.

"So do you, Harley. So do you." I brushed his hair from his forehead and bent down to give him a kiss. Harley sighed as our lips met and I pulled back slowly, caressing his cheek.

"Night, Harley Payne."

~*~

I woke up with a start and leaned over to look at the clock. I'd actually slept in. I sat on the edge of the bed and stretched my arms out, cracking my neck from side to side. I needed a good run. I dressed and headed down the stairs. Coffee was brewing and my mother sat at the table looking over recipes.

"Good morning, Achilles. Did you have fun last night?"

"Oh yes," I laughed, heading to the fridge. "Have you seen Harley?"

"He is down at the beach. He was up early," she informed me.

I peeked out the window, but saw no sign of him. That wasn't odd, though. With the amount of vines and trees that grew between the house and the beach, it wasn't uncommon for the view to be blocked.

"I'm going to head out for a run." I bent and kissed my mom's cheek.

I took the stairs down to the beach and looked in both directions. A figure sat by the water way at the other side of the beach. I headed that way and as I got closer, noticed that it was Harley. He was wearing shorts, sitting with his toes in the water. His shoes and socks were at his side. He looked up as I approached and a grin formed.

"Hey." Harley half-waved.

I finally got to him and plopped down in the sand.

"Were you running?" I asked.

"Yup. Got up early for some reason and felt the need. Must be all that alcohol in my system. Needed to run it out."

"Want to run with me?"

"Sure." Harley stood and I helped him as he put his socks and shoes back on. We ran together, side by side on the beach, the sun warming us. Being with Harley just felt...right. I thought back to when Mac approached me about a job. I didn't think I was ready to be a full-time bodyguard, but then I saw Harley's picture and read his story, and I couldn't have said no even if I wanted to. Something about him called to me; maybe it was his vulnerability or the sadness in his eyes. We stopped by the docks and both sat down, removing our shoes and dipping our feet in the water.

"How many girlfriends have you had, Harley?"

Harley scrunched his brows in thought. "Before I became famous or after?"

"Before."

"One or two. I wasn't really a one-chick kind of guy even then. I dated one girl for two weeks, and the second for one. I just couldn't devote my time to someone. Besides, I really didn't want them to see what my home life was like." Harley turned to me. "Was Brian the only guy you were with?"

"Yes." I nodded.

"Wow."

"I know. I'm so...inexperienced." I chuckled.

"When you said you'd wait for me...you know, until I was ready. Did you mean that?"

"Of course I did. Why?"

"I think when we get back home, I don't want to wait anymore."

I searched his eyes and the meaning behind what he'd said became very clear. I swallowed hard.

"Do you mean…you want to? Or you want me to?"

"Oh, I want to, maybe later you can take me. You do top, don't you? Or are you just a catcher? Because I gotta be honest here, I'd love to feel that."

My mouth dropped open and Harley wiggled his brows at me. I leaned forward until we were nose to nose.

"I have to warn you. I can get a bit rough," I said huskily.

"Damn," Harley breathed. "That's all kinds of sexy!"

"You are something else, Harley Payne," I laughed.

We spent the rest of the day with my parents. My father played chess with Harley and I sat on the couch with my mother. Harley was so happy here, I dreaded taking him back to Arizona. I wanted him to stay happy and carefree. My parents absolutely adored him, my mother wanted to adopt him. Harley was laughing with my father — real honest-to-goodness laughter, and my heart ached for him. He'd have to go back home and deal with the parents who birthed him then ignored him. My mother's hand slid into mine and I glanced over to see tears in her eyes.

"What is it, Mama?" I asked quietly.

"He deserves so much more," she said. "You make sure he gets it, Achilles. Do not let him push you away."

I searched my mother's eyes. "What is it?"

"I think it will get worse before it gets better."

"Well, I'll be with him no matter what."

"Take good care of each other, Achilles."

"I will."

~*~

We spent the next two days with my mom and dad. Harley went fishing with my father while I stayed with my mom and cooked. The next day, I was with my father fishing and Harley stayed with my mom. We bobbed on the ocean, our lines hanging over the side of the boat. The sky was clear with a slight breeze wafting through our hair. My father was resting on his elbows, face tilted to the sun. He looked so alive just then.

"I won't be around forever, Achilles," my father began, breaking the silence.

"And here I thought we could just have a relaxing day."

"Harley needs to grieve for his brother. The anger, sadness, and loneliness are just beneath the surface in his eyes. He hasn't fully grieved for his brother."

"I can't make him, Papa," I argued.

"He will break and you must let him." My father considered me carefully. "I spent the day with him right here on this boat and I could see it. He loves you."

"What? No. We haven't said anything to each other like that. We're just falling right now."

"Oh Achilles, you fell flat on your face." My father chuckled.

I had to laugh at that. My father was right. I was in love with Harley, but I wasn't going to push him. My father took my hands and searched my eyes.

"Remember your loss, the pain you endured when you were hurt. Harley will come crashing down and you have to let him. Understand? You can't help him."

"Papa…"

"No. You can't. He must fall and pull himself back up or he will never be the man he needs to be."

I hugged my father. "We'll come back soon, Harley and me, okay? If you need me, just call."

"We are here for you as well, Achilles. This is your home and Harley's now."

"I love you, Papa."

"You are my pride and joy, Achilles. Be the man I raised you to be."

I would. I didn't know if I could let Harley fall without running to catch him, though. If my father was right, I would have to.

Chapter 14
Achilles

I was draped over Harley, my body rutting against him as we kissed. He was so vocal, his hips lifting into mine. I had his hands pinned above his head on the couch as I ravished his mouth. Harley's whimpers were driving me fucking insane. I wanted to bend him over and fuck him, or he could bend me over. I really didn't give a shit at this point. We'd been coloring for the first half of the trip and, as soon as the flight attendant excused herself, Harley attacked me. This was so much better than worrying about crashing.

Harley bit my bottom lip and let it slide slowly out from between his teeth. A rumble rose from me and I sucked his tongue into my mouth. His hands went to my hips and then one slid down to the button on my jeans. His fingers fumbled and then he got the button off, pulling my zipper down low enough to get his hand in there. I gasped at the sensation of his warm fingers wrapping around my dick. We hadn't gone this far and my mind was racing as he started a slow stroke.

"Harley," I rasped, sucking in a breath when his thumb grazed the head of my dick.

"Hmm?" Harley licked at my lips, then nuzzled my neck, biting the flesh of my collarbone.

"Things are getting out of hand."

"Don't you want to join the mile high club?"

"The bathroom isn't small, but it's not *that* big."

Harley scooted out from underneath me and took my hand, hauling me up. We walked to the back of the plane and Harley opened the bathroom door, shoving me in. He closed the door behind us and stood there staring at me.

My pants were undone, the head of my dick poking out from behind my boxers. Harley fell to his knees and looked up at me as he took my boxers down, freeing my cock.

"What are you doing?" I asked with a tremble to my voice.

Harley just smiled and licked the head of my dick. My legs shook and I planted my hands on the bathroom walls as Harley sucked my cock down his throat. I wanted to cry out, but I bit my bottom lip instead and watched Harley's lips wrap around me and suck me down to my pubes. Holy. Fucking. Hell. I hadn't had head like that in…well, never. My hips bucked and I watched my dick slide in and out of Harley's mouth. My God, I couldn't tear my eyes away from the sight below me, Harley on his knees, my dick between his lips.

My balls drew taut and my fingers gripped the wall, and God help me, I couldn't stop fucking his mouth. Harley wrapped his fingers around my nuts and began earnestly deep throating me.

"Fuck…Harley, I'm going to fucking come. Pull off."

Harley shook his head and moaned around my dick. Vibrations skated down my shaft and I let loose a loud cry as I emptied into Harley's mouth, my hips still bucking as I did. Harley grabbed my ass cheeks and shoved me down, swallowing around me. I hung my head and tried to recapture my sanity as Harley stood up. His hands cradled my face and then he was kissing me. Our tongues met and curled around each other, I pulled Harley into me, grabbing his ass and hauling him up. His dick was rock hard against my abdomen and I slid my hand around and gave it a nice squeeze.

"Fuck yes," Harley groaned into my mouth.

"What do you want, Harley? You want me to suck you? Fuck you against the wall? Tell me what you want."

Harley leaned back a bit and stared at me. "I want you to suck me."

I pushed him up against the wall and took his mouth while I undid his jeans. They fell to the floor in a heap and I dropped to my knees just as he had and gripped his dick. I looked up at Harley from my position on the floor. His eyes were wild and black with desire. His hands threaded into my hair and I leaned forward, keeping eye contact with him as I tongued his slit, dipping in low and licking the precome from him.

His hips moved slowly and I opened my mouth, allowing him to control his thrusts. His fingers still gripping my hair, Harley pumped into my mouth, watching my face as he did. Our eyes held contact, never leaving each other, and I closed my lips around his girth. Harley's mouth was partially open, soft moans escaping from him as I increased the suction on him.

"Fuck, you look so sexy like that," Harley panted. "I'm going to come, Achilles. You can back off or take it. I'm negative."

I was going to take it. All of it. My tongue did a dance around his dick and Harley's eyes widened, his whole body went rigid, and then he was shouting, his cum spurting down my throat in bursts. I swallowed and licked the head of his dick as I pulled off. Harley slumped to the floor and I gathered him into my arms. He snuggled into me and breathed out a huge sigh.

"Wow. Best. Blow job. Ever."

"Yeah?" I grinned, kissing his temple.

"Hell yeah."

"We didn't fuck," I stated.

"Still counts, I think."

"Next time?"

"You're on."

~*~

We arrived at Harley's house and he unpacked. I checked the house again from top to bottom, but didn't see any signs of someone being there. Harley passed by me, letting his hand trail across my ass, and I shivered from the contact. We'd kissed the whole ride home after our bathroom excursion. That had to have been the shortest flight ever. I let Harley know I'd be in the shower while he finished unpacking. I wanted to wind down from the trip before I had to go back into bodyguard mode. Although I felt like I was so much more than that to Harley. At least I hoped I was.

Hot water cascaded over my head and my muscles began to relax under the spray. I tilted my head back and almost sighed in bliss as the jets pounded my sore muscles. I ran my hands through my hair and opened my eyes. Harley stood right in front of me, naked as the day he was born, and I think I drooled a little. A slow smile spread across his lips as he placed his hands on my chest. His hand slid up my pectoral muscle and snaked around my nape, pulling me down. Our lips met and I opened up immediately to Harley's mouth. He wrapped himself around me, deepening the kiss and rubbing his dick on my abdomen. He was hard, and fuck, so was I. We broke from the kiss, both of us panting, and Harley turned me around to face the wall. Fingers tickled down my back and then Harley's tongue slid down my spine. My body blew up in goosebumps as he trailed all the way down to the cleft of my ass.

I peered over my shoulder to see Harley's shit-eating grin as he nipped at my ass cheeks. Even now, he was playfully driving me insane. He kept his eyes on me as he slid a finger between my cheeks, rubbing my hole. I bit at my bottom lip and Harley let loose a feral rumble. A finger slid inside me and I instinctively spread my legs out, welcoming him in. My head hit the tile as Harley laved my nuts while he fingered my ass. The feeling of emptiness I had was being filled by one Harley Payne.

Harley's tongue slid up my back and he nibbled at my ear.

"I'd like to take this to the bed."

We quickly rinsed, dried off, and went to Harley's room. I stood at the foot of the bed while Harley ran his hands up my abdomen, his fingers tracing my scars.

"So much pain," Harley whispered.

He eased me back onto the bed and kissed his way up my body to my mouth. My eyes closed and I wrapped my arms around him as he deepened the kiss, his tongue dipping erotically into my mouth, savoring my taste just as I was savoring his. We broke from it, both breathing hard, our eyes locking. I could see my need reflected back in his eyes. I spread my legs out, welcoming him in and Harley reached across us, grabbing the tube of lube from his nightstand. Our eyes met again and I reached out to palm his face.

"I'm negative, too."

"I trust you." Harley leaned in to kiss me again while he lubed his fingers.

"No need." I stopped him, taking lube from his fingers and stroking his dick. I lifted my legs and nodded to him.

Harley positioned himself and kept eye contact with me as he pushed inside. His girth filled me and I gasped at the sensation of him bare. Harley's eyes widened as he pushed further inside, my walls clamped down on his cock, and I took a deep breath. Our foreheads touched and Harley kissed me.

"I'm sorry. Are you okay?" he whispered against my lips.

"I'm more than okay. God, you feel so good. Keep moving, you're not going to break me."

Harley pulled out a bit and then thrust back in. My back arched and I gripped his biceps as he found a rhythm and nailed my prostate. It took everything I had not to yell out loud as Harley slanted at an angle and slammed back into me. I wrapped my legs around his hips and moved with him, our mouths connected the whole time.

"God, this feels so fucking good. Love the way you feel," Harley rasped.

I felt like this was what I had been waiting for my whole life. Harley hadn't said he loved me, but the way he kissed me, I knew he did. I grabbed my dick and began jacking off as Harley's breathing became more labored. His hair fell in his eyes and he was biting at his bottom lip, fucking like a man on a mission. I knew the moment he came. His back stiffened and heat infused my whole body. I came with a shout, holding onto Harley as I did. He collapsed on me and burrowed into my neck as I held him. His whole body was shaking and he was wet with sweat. I smoothed his hair back and Harley tilted his head to look at me.

"You okay?" I asked.

"I'm perfect."

Harley fell asleep a few minutes later and I just laid there staring at the perfection next to me. He was...he was everything. I closed my eyes and Harley snuggled into my side, throwing a leg over me. This was what I wanted, and now I had it.

~*~

I woke up to Harley mumbling in my ear. I poked his side and his eyes opened and a slow smile graced his lips. He leaned in, kissed me, and I wrapped him up in my arms. His body was so warm and fit snuggly into mine.

"Hey." Harley kissed my chin and then bit it.

"Hungry?"

"I kinda am. How are you this morning?"

I wiggled my ass a bit and then smiled. "I'm good."

Harley chuckled and rolled out of bed. He threw some sweats on and held out a hand to me. "Come on. Let's go eat."

Harley and I talked over breakfast about going to the studio. I knew he wanted to get back to recording. He wasn't the kind of man who sat still for long. I cleaned up the dishes and Harley went to get dressed. I was just putting away the last dish when I heard a vehicle pull into the driveway.

"Someone's here. Be right back!" I called out.

I opened the door and stepped out, catching Axel jumping out of Gareth's Jeep. He held something in his hand and I walked over to him.

"What's up?" I asked.

"I wanted to wait until you got back."

I stopped walking and stared at him. "What is it?"

Axel ran a hand over his head and sighed audibly. "While you were gone, Harley's father called the cops and said Holden's bike was stolen."

"What?!"

"We took care of that, at least for now, but there's something else, Achilles, and you're not going to like it."

My skin broke out in a wave of chills as Axel glanced off to the side and fidgeted.

Oh God.

"Just tell me," I spat.

"At Gareth's request, as well as Jinx's, we looked into Holden's team and found out who was in charge after the fact. We got ahold of the guy and he said that Holden did write two letters because he packed them up himself along with Holden's personal effects."

"Okay…that's good news, right?"

Axel couldn't meet my eyes. I stepped forward. "What aren't you telling me?"

"Holden's team…the mission you went on that night you were ambushed, it was to retrieve a recon team that had been captured."

"Yes." I nodded slowly. The realization hit as Axel's eyes filled with sadness. "No…"

"I'm so sorry, Achilles."

"Holden died because we couldn't get to him," I barely whispered.

"You know you can't blame yourself for that. You and your team were ambushed! You almost died!"

"But I didn't, did I? I'm still here to breathe the fucking air!" I shouted.

"Achilles, you know how this works. There is nothing you could have done differently!"

"Well, I can do something now," I snapped. I ran to my truck and Axel followed me.

"Where are you going? Jinx is —"

"I'm going to get that fucking letter!"

~*~

I drove over the speed limit and cursed the whole way. I was the reason Holden Payne had died in the desert. Me. How the hell would Harley feel knowing that? I shook my head clear and concentrated on the road. I was going to get that letter come hell or high water. Harley deserved to know his brother had left him parting words. It was the least I could do for him. I pulled up next to the Payne house and took a deep, calming breath. I exited the truck and jogged up the walk to the front door. I could hear the TV on inside and knocked. I cocked my head to the side after a minute and knocked again. Louder this time. Footsteps sounded on the floor behind the door and then it flew open. I was looking right into the eyes of Harley's mother. She blinked and took me in.

"Yes?"

"I'm Achilles Castellanos, Harley's bodyguard? Can I please come in?"

"Oh, sure." She backed up a bit and I strode past her. "Can I get you a drink?"

"Water will be fine," I said as I walked around the living room. Pictures of Holden were everywhere. Not one of Harley among them. I balled my fists. I stopped in front of the flag in its case and peered at it closely.

"Here you are."

I turned to find Harley's mother holding a glass of water. I took it and thanked her as I perused the rest of the pictures.

"What can I do for you, Mr. Castellanos?"

"Well, you could start by handing over Holden's letter to Harley." I fixed her with a look.

"His what?" She asked nervously.

"Don't try to play stupid. I know full well you got two letters. I've got a guy who's willing to swear to it. So, I would advise you to hand it over."

"I don't know what you're talking about!" she shouted.

"Don't lie to me!" I threw my glass against the mantle and one of Holden's pictures came crashing down, hitting the floor. Glass shattered everywhere and Mrs. Payne gasped audibly. She rushed over to the picture and began picking up glass. I peered around her and noticed a white envelope sticking up behind the picture and the mat behind it.

"Stop!" I ordered. Her hands froze above the glass and I bent down and plucked the envelope from between the layers. Across the front, written in Holden's handwriting, I was sure, was one word.

Harley.

My hands shook as I turned it over and that was when I noticed it had been opened. Harley's mother stood on shaky legs and stared at the wall.

"How could you?" I whispered. "You opened it? This was a private letter from your son to his brother. How could you invade his privacy like that?"

Harley's mother hadn't moved. Still stared at the wall. I turned her around and lifted her face to mine.

"What kind of mother are you? To completely ignore the one remaining son you have? To keep this letter from him? To read Holden's last words to his brother? Who the fuck are you people?"

"Give that back!" she snapped.

"Oh, the hell I will. I'm giving this to Harley. And let me tell you something else — you want to act like he doesn't exist? Fine. Then he won't be paying *anything* for you anymore. The gravy train stops right here." I strode to the front door and looked back at her. "If I were you, I'd drop the charges against Harley because I bet his brother left him that bike in this letter." I shook it at her. "God help you."

"You have no right —"

"I have every right!" I shouted. "What did your letter say, huh? Something like 'stop ignoring Harley'? 'Be parents to him'? 'Love him'?" Harley's mother fidgeted and I glared at her. "Yeah, that's what I thought."

I stomped out of the house, slamming the door behind me. It had taken everything I had not to strangle her. I stared at the letter in my hand and then pocketed it in my jacket. I drove back to Harley's with a heavy heart. I knew he would be glad to finally have something from his brother, but my part in all this had to come out. I pulled up and cut the engine, contemplating what to do next. Axel's car was gone, and that meant I had to do this on my own. Harley ran out of the house just as I stepped onto the driveway.

"Where did you go?!" Harley yelled. "I was worried sick!"

I took Harley by the hand and led him into the house. I sat him down and kneeled in front of him. Harley took my hands, which were shaking, and looked into my eyes.

"You're freaking me out. Please talk to me," Harley whispered.

"I just came from your parents' house, Harley."

"Why?"

"Because your father filed charges against you for the theft of Holden's motorcycle."

"What?" Harley looked as though he'd been slapped by his father a second time.

I stood up and began pacing. I didn't know how I was going to tell Harley what assholes his parents were. Keeping something like this from him was just cruel. I stopped pacing and locked eyes with him.

"I told them you won't be paying anything for them anymore."

Harley jumped up. "What? Why would you do that?"

"Because of this." I pulled the envelope from my jacket and held it out for him to see. "They've had your letter all this time."

Harley stared at it, his hand twitching to touch it. I stepped closer and held it toward him. "Take it."

"You had no right," Harley whispered.

"I didn't? Probably not, but I was pissed. There's more, and you won't want to see me anyway after I tell you, so I guess I'll lay it all out. I'm the reason Holden died."

Harley's head snapped up. "What?!"

"It was my team that was supposed to rescue them, but we were ambushed ourselves and we never made it. That's why Holden died. We didn't get there in time to save him."

"Get out," Harley choked. "I can't handle all this right now!"

"I'm sorry, Harley. So very sorry."

I stepped out of the house, closing the door firmly behind me. I sent Hammer a text asking him to get to Harley's, then climbed into my truck. I drove blindly for a bit, not knowing where to go. I rolled my windows down and inhaled the fresh pine air. I stopped on the side of the road and closed my eyes. I felt a pinch at my neck and slapped my hand on it, only to come away with a dart between my fingers.

"Shit..."

Chapter 15
Harley

I stared at the letter in my hand, trying to process everything. My parents had kept Holden's letter from me? For three years, they'd kept it from me. I couldn't even process the other news Achilles had dropped into my lap because I was still focused on the letter in my hand. My name was written across the front in Holden's neat cursive. My heart was pounding in my chest. I didn't know what to do first. I sprung into action, grabbing my truck keys and walking out of the house.

I drove across town to the cemetery and pulled into the parking lot. My hand shook as I got out and walked to Holden's resting place. Flowers were drooping off to the side in a vase and I took them out, throwing them in a trashcan nearby. I sat down on the cold grass in front of his headstone and pulled the letter from my pocket. As I flipped it over, I noticed the seal was broken. Is that why Achilles had gotten so mad? I knew I was. They'd kept it from me *and* they'd read it?

I must have sat there for hours. Part of me wanted to read it so much and the other part was afraid of what would happen if I did. Every day was hard to get through without Holden and now I had his last words to me in my hand. I took a deep breath and pulled the paper out of the envelope. Opening it slowly, my eyes caught Holden's handwriting.

Harley,
If you're reading this, it means I'm gone; and God help me, I never wanted to leave you. I prayed every day that I'd make it through deployment, not for me, but for

you. I wanted to be there when you got married and had babies. I wanted to be crazy Uncle Holden. But I am gone, and I need you to know something. No matter how you felt, you were never a mistake in my eyes.

You were my miracle.

I loved you with every breath I took and I will keep loving you even after. You are a special human being and I am so proud to have been able to watch you grow up and become the man you are today. I want you to have my bike, Harley. It was always yours and I want you to think of us when you ride it. I will always be with you. You are never alone.

I see you.

I have always seen you.

All my love,

Holden

I couldn't see as tears rolled down my cheeks. A huge sob escaped me and then I was up, throwing whatever I could find.

"Why?! Why did you leave me all alone, Holden? You left me with *them*! You said you'd always be there! You said it!"

I fell to the ground and let it all out; my anger, the sadness, everything. I couldn't grab enough air and my nose was stuffed up. I sat back on my ass and wiped at my eyes.

"Well, it's about time."

My head snapped to the left to see Jinx standing across from me with his arms folded over his chest.

"Jinx?"

Jinx walked over to me and squatted down. He took my hand and palmed my cheek. "I'm so sorry."

"How did you know?" I asked.

"Axel." Jinx wiped my tears away. "I heard about Achilles, too. You can't blame him —"

"I don't." I sighed. "I know he couldn't have done anything. He almost died that night. Besides, Holden would be so mad at me if I did."

"Yes, he would." Jinx nodded in agreement.

"Why did they do this to me?" I snuffled, holding up the letter.

"I don't know." Jinx sat down next to me and we both stared at Holden's headstone. "What I *do* know is that Holden would never forgive you if you let someone like Achilles get away."

"He would tell me that Achilles is one hell of a fine piece of ass," I agreed.

I glanced over at Jinx to see a huge smile on his face. Our eyes met and we both busted out laughing.

"Yeah, he would." Jinx cracked up.

"I was more mad at him for interfering with my parents. If anyone is going to tell them they're cut off, it's me."

"Is that what you're going to do?"

"I don't know yet. I'm so fucking mad right now." I glanced over at Jinx. "What are you doing here anyway?"

"Well hell, I'll just go." Jinx made to stand up and I yanked him back down.

"Just tell me."

"Axel called after he got the info about Achilles and your brother. I was on the first plane out and just waiting for you to come home."

"Where's Jayden?"

"He's at the house with the rest of the London Boys."

I wrapped an arm around Jinx and leaned into him. "I'm so glad you're here."

"There's no place else I would be, Harley. You're my brother."

"From another mother." I grinned.

Jinx and I drove back to my house only to find Axel pacing back and forth in the driveway. I hit the garage door opener and pulled my truck inside. I hopped out and met with Jinx in the middle of the driveway. Axel motioned to us to come over to him.

"What's going on?" I asked.

"The rest of the guys are coming. Hammer's in the back yard."

I studied Axel's face closely. "What is it?"

"Inside. Now."

Jinx and I walked into the house and Axel went to the back yard to let Hammer in. Within a few minutes, Buster arrived along with Stan. I searched their faces for any sign of what could be going on, but none of them were giving anything away. Once Axel corralled everyone in the living room, he sat down and faced me.

"Where is Achilles?" he asked.

"I don't know. He left here hours ago. Why?"

"He's not answering his phone."

"Well, I might have gotten mad at him —"

"He would never not answer his phone, Harley," Hammer cut in.

"You think something happened? Maybe he got in an accident?" I stood up, clasping my hands. "Oh God, what if he's hurt?"

"Hammer." Axel nodded to the other bodyguard and I stopped pacing.

"What?" I asked.

"Achilles asked us to check the house once you left. We did. We found a partial print on your window, along with hair follicles. We checked the food in the fridge and had it all checked. Your milk contained arsenic."

"My milk?" I sat down in confusion. "Someone tried to poison me?"

"We're running the prints. The hair was blond but with a black root. We also found another print on your milk jug, still partial, but we can work with it."

"What is this? *CSI Arizona*?" Stan stood up and ran his hands over his face. "What the hell is going on here?"

"Oh God," I swallowed hard. "If anything happened to Achilles… I yelled at him. The last words I spoke to him were in anger."

"Hey." Axel moved to my side. "Achilles is well trained, Harley. We'll find him, I can promise you that."

"Blonde with black roots," Stan mumbled. "Have you had any contact with anyone out of the ordinary? You know, like someone not from town, Harley?"

"Um, the only person I've seen is Arielle at the bar. She's blonde and in need of a dye job."

"Arielle is here in Flagstaff?" Jinx asked in astonishment. "Why?"

"Said she was visiting someone."

"Who?" Axel asked.

"She didn't say, Rebel showed up and she left." I furrowed my brows. "I was sick right after that. I remember feeling hot and, well, weird."

"Roofie?" Hammer asked Axel.

"Sounds like it." Axel nodded.

"Do we have any pictures of her?" Buster asked.

"I don't think so," Stan said. "I can call Sebastian Lowery and see if he has any from the party at his house."

"Okay, get on that." Axel began to pace again.

"What if something happened, Jinx?" I whispered. "I can't lose him, too."

"Achilles will be fine." Jinx tried to soothe me.

Axel called Gareth and he showed up with Ransom and Rebel. We all sat together, all of them trying to keep me calm. Inside, I was anything but. I wanted to hear Achilles' voice, see his face and touch him. I needed to know he was all right.

"Sebastian says he doesn't have any pictures matching Arielle's description," Stan announced.

"Wait!" I stood up. "She said something about auditioning for Sal Falco's movie. Wouldn't they have something?"

Stan got back on the phone and relayed the info to Sebastian. He hung up and faced all of us.

"Sebastian said he'd call Sal and have him call us. So for now, we wait."

I watched the second hand on the clock as it ticked agonizingly slow. I felt like every second we wasted, something bad was happening to Achilles. I closed my eyes and prayed that he was okay. All of the bodyguards were hunched over laptops, going over the evidence they'd found. Stan's phone rang and he answered it immediately. He motioned to the laptop on the table.

"Ransom, check your email," Stan said.

We all looked over at Ransom and he shrugged, getting up and typing his password in. We all waited on pins and needles for the file to open. There was a glossy black and white headshot of Arielle and her audition tape.

"Thank you, Sal. We appreciate it," Stan told him, then hung up. "He said if we need anything else, don't hesitate to call him."

"Do any of you know her last name?" Stan regarded us all.

We all looked at each other and shook our heads.

"None of you? You've all fucked her — ugh, never mind." Stan sighed in exasperation.

"Hey, hold up!" Buster raised a hand in front of his own laptop. "Something is coming in on the fingerprint."

Hammer leaned in over Buster's shoulder.

"Adrianna Henderson?" Hammer turned to look at us.

I gasped. "Holy shit! We went to school with her! I dated her for like, two weeks!"

"What the fuck? She had plastic surgery for sure." Jinx stared at the picture.

"Well, she's got a record." Buster turned the laptop towards us. "She was caught with a guy who was carrying dope. She got community service and he went to jail. Her parents are still here in town. Dad's a veterinarian?"

"Get the address, Buster. We're going right now."

"I'm coming with you." I stood up.

"That's not an option, Harley —"Axel began.

"The fuck it isn't!" I practically snarled. "I'm going with you, no arguments!"

"Um, I'd listen to him, hon." Gareth poked his husband in the side.

"Fine." Axel folded his arms. "If I tell you to do something, you do it. Got it?"

"Let's go." I trudged by him.

The four of us drove to the Henderson's house. I was hoping she'd be there with Achilles. What the hell? My ex tried to poison Achilles and me and now she might have taken him? What if she hurt him? The sun was setting as we pulled up to a two-story in a quiet residential neighborhood. Hammer and Buster got out, both drawing guns and disappearing in different directions. I followed behind Axel as he drew his own gun and walked to the front door. He rang the doorbell and an elderly gentleman answered, looking at Axel as if he were the grim reaper.

"Dr. Henderson?" Axel asked.

"Yes? Who are you?"

"We're looking for your daughter, Dr. Henderson. Have you seen her?"

"Are you cops? What has she done now?" The old man sighed.

"Can we come in?" Axel asked, placing his gun back in his waistband.

The old man gestured behind him wearily and we entered the house. Axel walked to the back door and opened it, allowing Hammer and Buster in. The two of them took off to inspect the house while we dealt with the father.

"I haven't seen her in two days. She said she had stuff to do. I'm missing a dart gun from my clinic."

"You have dart guns?" I asked.

"Yes, for the bigger animals. I get called when someone's injured an elk or a bear and they have to sedate it. I'm part of the park's animal control as well, so I get called in a lot. We had an incident with an elk on the Eighty-nine and I was called out, but I couldn't find my gun."

"She knocked him out." Axel glanced over at me.

"Who knocked whom out?" Adrianna's father asked.

"Your daughter," I answered. "Where would she go? Do you know?"

"We have a cabin up in Snow Bowl, she could have gone there."

"Could you give us the address?" Axel asked him.

"Sure."

Hammer and Buster joined us, both shaking their heads.

"She's not here." Hammer put his gun away.

"No, she's not. But we may have a lead."

~*~

It was getting dark and cold, and once again, I worried over what could be happening to Achilles. I sent up a silent prayer to Holden to watch over my man.

My man.

Yes, Achilles was mine. He'd been mine from the moment he was introduced to me. I would never forget that day as long as I lived. He had such patience with me, chasing me around Europe when I was half-clothed and drunk off my ass. I was going to make sure he knew how I felt the moment we found him.

I just hoped we found him very soon.

Chapter 16

Achilles

My eyes opened slowly and a shape was sitting across from me. I licked at my dry lips and tried to focus. Blonde hair came into focus and blue eyes narrowed as I finally opened my eyes all the way. The chick from the party was sitting across from me in sweats and a T-shirt. I tried to move my hands and realized they were zip-tied to the chair I was sitting in and my feet were bare.

"Arielle?" I croaked out.

"Well, look who finally woke up. Sorry about that, but I guess I used too much ketamine."

"What?" I blinked.

"My dad's a vet here in town. I kinda stole his dart gun. It was the only way to get you."

"Why?"

Arielle snorted and waved a hand in the air.

"Please! I've seen you with Harley. Did you know he and I dated in high school? Oh yeah, for two weeks, then he told me he didn't want me to meet his family and ended it. Just like that." Arielle snapped her fingers. "I came to town right after I saw him in California when he basically snubbed me. He's been all up in your shit since you've come back to town. Harley's gay, wouldn't you know it? All of them are, I bet! He used me for sex like some cheap whore! I wanted him to pay."

"What did you do?" I asked slowly.

"I was at the diner that night, visiting a friend. I might have slipped a little something in your food," Arielle beamed.

"Harley ate half my food!"

"How did that go?" Arielle sat forward and clasped her hands together. "Did you have a wonderful night? See, arsenic is hard to find in your body, you actually have to be looking for it."

"You poisoned us?"

"Well, that was meant for you, but oh well." Arielle shrugged.

I lurched forward in the chair with a growl and Arielle jumped up, backing away from me.

"I roofied him at the club too, but I guess he still wasn't feeling well from all that poison."

I pulled at my zip ties and Arielle squatted quite a few feet away from me.

"I wouldn't struggle too hard, you might hurt yourself."

"If I get out of these…" I threatened.

"You'll what?" Arielle laughed.

I closed my eyes and exhaled slowly. I allowed the rage in, and the darker side of me began to rise.

"You wouldn't hurt a woman," Arielle cackled.

I opened my eyes slowly and locked on hers. "It wouldn't be the first time, sweetheart," I said calmly.

Arielle backed away from me and darted looks at the door. "You're lying."

"You are dry humping my last nerve. Who do you think I am? Just a bodyguard? Do you even know what I did for a living before this? I was a sniper and I killed people, do you get that? I killed women, Arielle. Women with bombs strapped to their bodies, intent on taking out American troops. So don't think for one second I won't snap your neck, especially if you try to hurt Harley in any way."

Arielle pulled a syringe from her back pocket and I struggled in the chair. She jabbed it into me and backed away quickly. I hissed through my teeth and she ran for the door, opening it. She cast a look at me as she left. I slumped back and closed my eyes again as she closed the door. I waited for her to leave, making sure the car's engine was far away before I tried to get free.

My feet were free of ties, so I stood up and positioned the chair against the wall. Hauling my body as far as I could away from it, I whipped back and broke one of the arms on the wall. Wood splintered and I pulled my hand free. I pulled all the drawers out in the kitchen until I found a pair of scissors and cut myself free. I searched for my phone, but couldn't find it. I had to warn Harley and the guys. I searched the house for a phone but didn't find one. I opened the front door to see snow on the ground. Where I was, I had no clue. I rifled through the cabinets and found some water bottles and some crackers. I stuffed them in a plastic bag and then grabbed four more plastic bags.

I headed upstairs and checked all the closets for clothing, but found them bare. Then I checked the linen closet. I grabbed two thick towels and wrapped them around my feet, placing the plastic bags over them and tying them up. I covered my hands as well as my head, and ventured outside. I had no idea when the crazy bitch would be back and I didn't want to be there when she returned.

I checked the sky for the North star and headed the opposite direction. As I headed down the mountain, I could barely see lights way off in the distance. At least I knew I was heading toward town. The temperature was dipping lower as I kept a good pace through the trees. My feet were cold, as were my hands, but I knew they would hold out a little while longer. I stopped and took a small sip of my water and ate a cracker. I needed to stay focused. Whatever she'd injected me with would definitely start to fuck with me once my adrenaline wore off. I could feel it already. I was starting to sweat and my eyesight was getting blurry. The ground rushed up to meet my face and I spit out snow, trying to haul my weary body back up. The temperature was starting to take its toll on my body as I stood up again and began walking. I kept my eyes trained on the terrain ahead, imagining Harley's smile as I did. What I wouldn't give to see it one last time. I could barely make out lights up ahead. I wasn't sure what the hell I was seeing, they seemed to be bouncing around. I fell again, my legs giving out. I rolled to my back and stared at the moon in the sky.

"Achilles?!"

Now I was hearing things. Shit.

"Achilles? Where are you?"

"Harley?" I whispered.

"Achilles? Where are you?"

Harley sounded frantic, and then I heard Hammer far off in the distance. I tried to shout, but my voice wouldn't cooperate. I rolled back to my stomach and got on my hands and knees and began to crawl.

"Harley!" I rasped.

"Achilles? Keep talking! I'm coming!" Harley shouted, "Guys! He's over here!"

"Harley, I'm so sorry," I grated.

Light shone in my eyes and I lifted my head. Harley slid onto his knees and wrapped his arms around me tightly.

"Oh God! I thought she killed you!" Harley sobbed into my neck.

"I'm hard to kill," I mumbled into his hair. "So sorry, Harley."

"Shut up, stop apologizing and look at me."

Harley lifted my face to his and peppered kisses all over my lips, eyes, and cheeks.

"C-c-cold," I chattered out as I shivered.

Hammer and Buster appeared in front of me with what looked like a blanket, and Buster picked me up while Hammer wrapped it around me. It was so warm. I closed my eyes and felt a hand slip into mine.

"We've got you, Achilles," Harley whispered.

"Arielle…" I started.

"We know, Axel is out hunting her now," Hammer reassured me.

I had to laugh at the word "hunting" because it was what we all said when looking for a suspect. My laughter turned into tears as I realized what could have happened to Harley if Arielle wasn't caught. Harley placed a soft kiss on my lips and caressed my cheek.

"We've got you now. I'm never letting you go, Achilles."

"Stavros." I held Harley's hand.

"What?" Harley bent in closer.

"My middle name," I mumbled.

"Okay, stay with me, Achilles." Harley placed a kiss on my temple. "Stay with me."

"So tired." I closed my eyes and sighed.

"Achilles! Stay with me!"

"Harley…"

I was put into a truck and Harley had my head in his lap. He was warming my face with his hands and I grabbed one, placing a kiss on his palm.

"Don't close your eyes!" Harley placed my hand on his cheek. "Don't leave me, Achilles, please? Please don't leave me alone."

I wiped a tear from his cheek and licked it from my fingers.

"Never alone, Harley. I will always be with you." I closed my eyes and tried to concentrate on breathing.

"Achilles! Guys, hurry!"

Chapter 17
Achilles

I opened my eyes slowly and stared at the ceiling above me. Soft light illuminated the room and beeping was coming from somewhere. My hand was warm and I looked down to see Harley's hand in mine. He was asleep on the side of the bed. I wiggled my fingers and his head sprang up. He wiped at his eyes and blinked, focusing on me.

"You're awake," he said quietly. "I was worried when you didn't wake up."

"What happened?" I heard myself asking. My throat was raw and my voice rough.

"Hammer, Buster and I found you in the woods. You'd wrapped your feet and hands, but you still had a mild case of frostbite. The doctor wanted to keep you a few days because of the drugs in your system."

"Arielle!" I tried to sit up and Harley placed a hand on my chest, pushing me back gently.

"Axel got her. Please calm down. You're safe."

"I wasn't worried about me, I was worried about you." I touched his cheek.

"I'm so sorry I yelled at you, Achilles. I was just so…freaked out."

"It's okay, I understand. You don't have to stay with me. I know how you must feel."

"Do you really? Because I wanted to slap the shit out of you when you kept babbling about taking Holden's place. Do I miss my brother? Yes, of course. Would I want him back? Of course, but to say you'd gladly take his place so I could have him back? Not gonna happen. You are stuck with me, Achilles Stavros Castellanos."

I blinked and focused on his face. Harley smirked and I groaned. "Shit, I told you my middle name?"

"Yes, and I love it." Harley leaned over and placed a soft kiss on my lips. "I'm not leaving you. You scared the shit out of me. I was so worried about you and then I wanted to kick my own ass for yelling at you. God, if those were the last words you ever heard from me, I'd have lost my mind."

I palmed Harley's cheek and searched his eyes. They were so light just then, like melted caramel and chocolate. He was such a sight for sore eyes. I pulled him close and our lips met. Harley whimpered a bit and wrapped his arms around me carefully.

"I'm so sorry I yelled at you," he breathed across my lips.

"I'm sorry I couldn't save your brother. I'm sorry I yelled at your parents. I'm not sorry I met you, though. You are the best thing that has ever happened to me, Harley James Payne."

Harley grinned and ran a fingertip over my lips.

"I went to the cemetery. I cried and I yelled and screamed."

"You feel better?" I asked.

"Yes, I do. I don't know what I'm going to do about my parents just yet. One day at a time."

"I'm glad you finally got to grieve properly, Harley." I glanced around the room and noticed it was dark out. "Just how long have I been here?"

"Two days. I want you to come home with me. Is that okay?"

"It's perfect."

~*~

The following morning, I was still not allowed to get up without help. My feet were still a little sore, but they were looking much better according to the doctor. I stumbled trying to get out of the bathroom and Harley was right at my side in an instant. I kissed the top of his head as he walked me slowly back to my bed. He hadn't left my side since I woke up. He looked a little tired, but he'd been sleeping with me in the hospital bed and I was kind of big.

"You can go home, you know." I raised a brow at him.

"Not without you." Harley pulled the covers up over me and sat on the edge of the bed.

"Harley, about what I said to your parents —"

"Don't." Harley raised his hand. "You were right, but I wanted to say it myself."

"I want you, Harley Payne." I took his hand.

"Yeah? Even though I'm nuts and run around half-naked?"

"I love it when you run half-naked." I wiggled my brows.

"If you're a good boy, I'll run around buck naked."

Clapping erupted behind us and Harley turned around. Jinx stood in the doorway with Jayden and Rebel. The three of them walked in and Rebel leaned over my tray of food, sniffing.

"What the fuck is that?" He pointed at the tray.

"No idea. How are you, Rebel?" I asked.

"Fisting and existing my friend." Rebel winked.

I choked and Jinx slapped Rebel on his back. Harley and Jayden burst into laughter.

Within the hour, I had a whole roomful of people. Jayden's bandmates had come, as well as Hammer, Buster and Stan. Ransom and Gareth were on their way with Axel. I looked at all the people in my room and then zeroed in on Harley talking with Jinx in the corner. Harley was laughing and smiling. Our eyes met and he gave me a shit-eating grin.

"I thought we'd lost you," Hammer said, sitting on the bed. "As much as we wanted to join in on the hunt for Arielle, both Buster and I wanted to find you first. You're like our little brother." Hammer mussed my hair. "Harley was beside himself. I don't think I've ever seen him pissed off, but boy *was* he when he found out about Arielle, a.k.a. Adrianna."

"Thank God for cold weather training, huh?" I joked.

"Take a few days off, okay? We'll be fine while you rest up."

I nodded and leaned back in the bed. Hammer glanced over his shoulder and I sat up a bit to see what he was looking at. I spotted Jayden and his guys in the corner, talking with Stan.

"Marc?" Hammer turned to me and I searched his eyes. "What is it?"

"What is what?"

"Who are you looking at?" I tried to peek around him again.

"No one. Rest up."

Harley came back over to the bed and climbed in next to me. "Ready to go home?"

"More than ready."

~*~

Harley opened the door for me and I stepped over the threshold, looking around nervously. I knew they'd caught Arielle, well, Adrianna, and she'd been put away, but my innate need to protect Harley was always front and center. I was feeling ten times better and ready to get back to my life. Now that I had Harley in my life as a boyfriend, things were much different. I overheard him in the hall when they were discharging me, asking about what he needed to do for his boyfriend. I smiled at the memory and Harley came to stand in front of me, tilting his head in question.

"I heard you call me your boyfriend," I admitted.

"I did." Harley nodded. "Was that okay?"

"More than okay."

"Let's get you off your feet, okay?" Harley wrapped an arm around me and helped me down the hallway to his room. I stopped as we walked through the door and stared at the wall across the way. A picture I had colored was in a frame hanging on the wall.

"You framed it?" I whispered.

"It's an original Castellanos." Harley stepped in front of me and held my face in his hands. "This house is just as much yours now. I want you to be comfortable."

"Harley…" I started.

"No. You be quiet and get in that bed." Harley pointed to it. "I talked to your parents and assured them you are fine, but I still want you to get on the computer so they can see you for themselves."

"Yes, sir!" I reclined on the bed and Harley fluffed the pillows behind me. "Could you wear a nurse's outfit?"

"Ha. Very funny." Harley sat down on the edge and took my hand. He laced our fingers together and then raised my hand to his lips, kissing the back of it. "You scared me so badly."

"I'm not leaving you, Harley. Not ever. Not while I still breathe," I assured him.

"I wanted to tell you when I found you —" Harley's phone beeped and he grabbed it, staring at the screen. "It's Stan."

"Take it."

Harley answered and I kept hold of his hand. Whatever Stan was saying, Harley nodded his head and did a lot of the "uh huhs" before hanging up. He placed his phone down and then looked at me.

"Stan booked us on a Christmas special for an LGBT youth fundraiser. The guys from Black Ice and Ivory Tower are on it as well. It's in California. You up for a little trip?"

"I will be."

"Okay, but for now, I want you to rest." Harley leaned in and kissed me lightly. He pulled back slightly, our lips still touching. "And when you feel better, I want you to take me."

I backed up and searched his eyes. "Are you sure? I mean, you've never —"

Harley placed a finger over my lips.

"Yes, I'm sure, more than ever now. When I thought something happened to you, that maybe I'd never see you again, something snapped inside me." Harley cradled my face in his hands. "I love you, Achilles."

"Are you sure?" I whispered.

"Oh yeah, I'm sure. When I wake up, the first person I want to see is you. When I color an awesome picture, you're the first one I want to show it to. I want to take walks on the beach with you in Greece and drink Ouzo out of your belly button."

I laughed and Harley grinned. He sobered and stared into my eyes.

"I love you, Achilles Stavros Castellanos. Completely."

"I love you too, Harley. From the first second I saw you, I knew you'd be trouble."

"Yes, but aren't I fun?" Harley wiggled his brows.

I grabbed him, throwing him on his back and hovering above him. I looked down into the face of the man who had stolen my heart from the second I walked into that dressing room at Wembley Stadium. Harley's first question that day had been to ask me if my mom actually named me Achilles. I smiled at the memory and Harley cocked his head to the side, smiling at me.

"What is it?" he asked.

"I'm remembering the first day I met you. Seems so long ago now."

"I just remember thinking how appropriate your name was." Harley pulled me down. He wrapped himself around me and nuzzled my neck.

"I'm glad you finally got your letter, Harley," I murmured.

"You said the same thing Holden did." Harley leaned back and met my eyes. "That's how I know it's you, Achilles. It will always be you. You *see* me."

I palmed his face and smiled. "And I always will."

Chapter 18
Achilles

California was sunny and warm, a huge difference from Flagstaff. Christmas was just days away and I was making sure Harley's gift was coming along nicely. I'd taken him to the doctor to have his stitches removed and he was given a clean bill of health. Harley was holding my hand as we entered the hotel. Jinx and the rest of the guys were right behind us. Jayden's London Boys guys had come along with us as they were playing in the show as well. Ransom was laughing with the Spiros twins as we hit the check-in desk. I was feeling ten times better, my body recovering nicely from my ordeal in the woods.

"Well, well, if it isn't the Skull Blasters."

I turned, along with the rest of the guys, to see Tony Wilcox, keyboardist for Ivory Tower, standing behind us.

"I hear you and I are going to be playing piano, Jinx." Tony stuck his hand out.

"That's what I hear." Jinx shook the hand and pulled Tony into a bro-hug.

"No Backstreet Boys this time, though. Eh?" Tony ribbed Jinx.

"No need." Jinx motioned to Jayden. "Got my boy-bander right here."

"It's good to see you guys!" Tony shook all the guys' hands, then stopped on me. "So, you wrangled Harley?"

"In more ways than one." I grinned, extending my hand.

"Well, I'll see you guys later at practice? Sebastian said they had a poll online with six songs, and the public gets to pick what we're all playing together. Should be interesting." Tony regarded all the guys and then waved. "See ya soon!"

Harley squeezed my hand and I looked down at him. "What is it?"

"Can we see Paul while we're here?" he asked.

"Of course." I nodded.

"Okay, well, let's get unpacked and get to the studio. I'm curious to see what we'll be doing. I'm so excited, though!"

I had to smile at Harley's enthusiasm. He was so childlike at times. It was one of the traits that made him so damned loveable. We went to the room and unpacked, and then headed back downstairs to the waiting van. I slipped in the back with Buster and Hammer and reclined, letting out a soft sigh. Hammer nudged me and I opened my eyes to see him smiling at me.

"What?" I asked, suspicious.

"I saw this coming the first day. Buster and I had a bet."

"Yep," Buster chimed in. "I gave it a year; Marc had 6 months. He won."

"You bet on my love life?" I glared at them both.

"You're talking again!" Jinx shouted at us.

Hammer grunted and folded his arms, as did Buster.

"Aw man! Come on!" Gareth pouted. "You can't go back to being quiet now!"

I looked from Buster to Hammer and laughed. "Sorry guys, but I heard you were very vocal when I went missing."

"Fine," Hammer balked. "But don't expect it all the time."

"Hey," Harley started as he leaned over the back of the seat. "Will you guys sing?"

"No," they both answered in unison.

I laughed.

We hit the studio and I sat in the front row as all the guys assembled center stage, waiting for Sebastian. Harley had his guitar in one hand with his back to me, and fuck if he wasn't hotter than hell from the back. He was even hotter from the front. I chuckled softly and Harley glanced over his shoulder at me with a grin.

"Um, excuse me?"

I looked up to see one of Jayden's band mates standing in front of us. He was looking from me to Hammer to Buster.

"I'm Evander," he continued. "One of the roadies hurt his back and I was wondering if you could maybe help with the amps?"

"I'll go." Hammer stood up immediately.

Buster and I stared at him and he shrugged, following Evander backstage. Buster threw a look at me and I raised my hands in an "I don't know" gesture.

Sebastian hit the stage and let the guys in on what was going on and what the public had chosen. I smiled as he revealed what song they were all going to play together. "November Rain" by Guns N' Roses. I could actually see them all playing that together. The finalist from last season's *Singers* would be there as well, with his runner-up. They had formed a band together and were already rocking the charts from what Jinx had told us. They would be closing the show with Sophie B. Hawkins "Damn, I Wish I Was Your Lover" and Tesla's "Love Song." I really couldn't wait to hear it.

Jinx and Tony sat at grand pianos, facing each other, and Harley and Gareth were with the guitarists from Black Ice and Ivory Tower. I loved watching Harley play. He and

Gareth together were fucking amazing, but add in the other guys? It was phenomenal. For five hours, I sat with Buster and Hammer while the guys rocked it out onstage. I'd never seen Harley so sexy, his hair and shirt were soaked with sweat and his brow was creased in concentration.

Sebastian called a halt to the day and Harley bounded down the stairs and right into my arms. I held him close and inhaled his scent.

"Wanna go shower with me?" He grinned.

"Was that a real question?" I answered.

I swear Harley actually ran back to the room, dragging me along with him. He quickly swiped the key and pulled me into the room, attacking my lips. I wrapped him up tightly in my arms and returned his fevered kisses. I loved the taste of him, knew I'd never get tired of it. Harley was what my mother would call "my lobster." The one just for me.

"Agapi mou," I murmured against his lips.

Harley pulled back a bit and searched my eyes. "What does that mean?"

"It means my love in Greek. You are kardia mou and psihi mou—my heart and my soul."

"Will you teach me Greek?"

"Yes. Of course."

"I want to be able to talk to your parents." Harley beamed.

"You talk to them now."

"You know what I mean." Harley leaned in and kissed me again.

I stripped him down and dragged him into the shower with me. Harley was all over me, his lips nibbling at mine, tongue sliding erotically over my lips. I was in sensual overload with him and I fucking loved it. Harley slid down my body and dropped to his knees in front of me. I cupped his cheek and our eyes met. Damn, he looked so fucking good on his knees, my dick right at his lips. Harley swiped the head of my dick and I grabbed the wall immediately as he sucked me down. The guy was really good at that. My hips bucked into his mouth as he upped his tempo and swallowed me down. I came with my fingers gripping the tile, almost shouting through my release. Harley licked through my slit, then licked his lips and stood up. I grabbed his nape and pulled him into a kiss. Harley rocked against me as I basically fed from him.

"Let me take care of you," I murmured.

"Nope. Already came." Harley smiled shyly.

"Really?"

"Yep. Just hearing you." Harley shivered. "Turns me on."

I licked his lips and pulled him in again. Harley melted into me and I took my damn time feasting on him. We pulled away from the kiss and Harley tilted his head, staring at me. "You need to go to bed. I can tell you're tired."

"Well, you sucked the energy from my body."

"Come on, big guy." Harley turned the water off and helped me out. He dried me off and then took me to the bed. I crawled in and rolled to my side, lifting the covers and inviting him in. Harley got in and wrapped his arms around me, placing his head on my chest.

"I love listening to your heart," Harley whispered. "Sometimes, I swear it beats in time with mine."

"Because it does." I played with his hair as he snuggled into me further, placing his ear above my heart.

"I want you to read Holden's letter to me."

"Are you sure? That's really personal, Harley."

Harley lifted his head and met my eyes. "Yes. I think you need to read it. When you said you saw me, it meant so much to me and then Holden…" Harley swallowed hard and I brought him in close to me.

"He was a very special man, Harley. He saw what I see. You are so full of light and love. I'm so warm when I'm with you. Does that make sense?"

"Yes, it does." Harley sighed against my chest. "Because that's how I feel when I'm with you."

Harley fell asleep and I continued to run my fingers through his hair. I kissed the top of his head and closed my eyes. I wished Harley's parents could truly see him the way Holden and I did. Everyone who spent even a little time with Harley Payne could see he was caring. Even after being treated the way he was, he still had hope for his parents. I guess I couldn't fault him for that. I didn't know what I would have done if my parents ever treated me that way. Harley mumbled into my chest and I lifted his face to mine, placing a soft kiss on his lips.

"Love you," Harley murmured in his sleep.

My chest tightened and I kissed him again.

"I love you too, Harley Payne," I whispered.

I woke up alone and quickly sat up, throwing a glance around the room. I didn't hear the shower and there was no sign of Achilles anywhere. I hopped out of bed and checked the room from top to bottom. On the desk by the phone was a note, and I could see Achilles' neat script.

Didn't want to wake you, went to the gym. Be back soon, agapi mou.
Achilles

I couldn't stop the smile spreading across my face as I read it again. I felt like a giddy teenager. I jumped in the shower and let the showerhead massage my body, my mind full of Achilles. It seemed as if my life was finally turning around. I was in love with a great guy and had a career I enjoyed. Now if I could just get my parents to actually admit they had another son, life would be golden. I stepped out of the shower and stopped in my tracks. Achilles stood in the middle of the room naked, practicing some kind of martial art moves. He was so damn graceful for his height and size, it never ceased to amaze me.

I leaned against the wall and just watched him. Scars peppered his arms, legs, and thighs, as well as his chest, but to me, they were a daily reminder of what Achilles endured and survived. And if he could go through all that and remain who he was, then I needed to stop focusing on what I didn't have, and concentrate on what I did. Achilles turned in my direction and he stretched his arm out fully, motioning to me with his fingers. I walked to him and he placed me in front of him, running his hand down my arm to my fingers. He threaded them together, and then began to move us as one.

"What are we doing?" I whispered.

"Tai Chi Chuan. Just move with me."

I closed my eyes and just moved with Achilles, matching my breathing to his. A sense of peace washed over me and I began to move effortlessly along with him. Our chests rose and fell together, our bodies in sync. I'd never felt so close to another human being before. I had no idea how much time went by, but Achilles moved to stand up straight and brought our hands together. We both bowed, keeping our heads at shoulder level, and then broke apart. I turned to see Achilles wiping sweat from his brow. He was fucking glorious naked.

"I'm going to shower." Achilles kissed the top of my head as he crossed the room to the bathroom.

"Will you teach me that, too?" I called after him.

"Anything you want."

I snickered at that and heard his laugh from the bathroom. I couldn't help it, he was just so damned sexy. My phone pinged and I grabbed it off the nightstand. I had a message from Calli. I smiled as I read it.

Good luck with the LGBT special! So proud of you! Kisses to you and Achilles.

Mom.

I wiped at my eyes at that one word.

Mom.

Achilles' mom was more of a mother to me than my own. I texted her back and then laid back on the bed, staring at the ceiling. Achilles leaned over me, resting his hands on either side of my head. I hadn't even heard him get out of the shower.

"Hey." He leaned down and kissed my nose. "What's wrong?"

I wrapped my arms around his neck and pulled him down, kissing him. Achilles responded right away and I arched up into him, rubbing myself all over his lower body. Achilles broke from the kiss and eyed me.

"You okay?"

"I'm fine. Ready to go eat?"

"Yep." Achilles pulled me up and enveloped me in his arms.

"Oh, your mom texted. She said she's proud." I leaned back to meet eyes with Achilles.

"Yeah? She really does love you. I think if she could, she'd trade me for you."

"Nah. But it's a nice thought." I took his hand and walked to the door. "Let's head down and see who's up."

~*~

I headed for the buffet as Achilles went to find the gang. I loaded up a plate for myself and then loaded one for Achilles as well, making sure it had a ton of fruit on it. I headed back to the dining room to find Achilles surrounded by the guys, his phone up for all to see. I furrowed my brows as I approached the table and the unmistakable sound of my voice floated on the air. I groaned as I recognized the song. My karaoke night was being played for the guys.

"Really, Achilles?" I set the plates down.

"What? At least you're clothed," he retorted.

"Nice, Harley." Jinx wrapped an arm around Jayden and leaned back with a grin. "The Tubes?"

"Shut up." I pointed at him with a croissant.

"So, Sebastian has informed us that rehearsals start at noon today." Jinx bit into a blueberry muffin and Jayden stole the rest of it from him. "So what's on the agenda until then? Jayden wants to hit the beach."

"I'm going to go see Paul," I announced, sitting down.

"Speaking of Paul," Ransom piped up. "If it's okay with you guys, I think I'm going to spend Christmas with him. He shouldn't be alone."

"No, you're right," I said. "Paul should have at least one of us with him. When are you going to transfer him to Arizona?"

"Probably in January, after the New Year. His doctor says he's doing very well," Ransom informed us.

"Well, let's eat and head out." I pushed Achilles' plate in front of him and pointed at it. "Eat."

~*~

The hospital was decorated to the nines in holiday cheer. A huge Christmas tree stood in the middle of the waiting room with tinsel brushing the floor. Everywhere, there were holiday candles, and mistletoe hung from the ceiling. Achilles and I signed in and then were led out to the garden. Paul was seated against a large tree with a book in his hand. The waterfalls gurgled around us as we approached him.

"Hey, Paul," I called out.

He looked up and a large smile formed on his face. He set the book down and stood to receive my embrace.

"Harley! God, it's good to see you!" Paul enthused.

"Good to see you, too. Ransom said he's springing you to a new place next month."

"That's what he said." Paul nodded. "I'm looking forward to it. Not that I don't like this place, but I miss Arizona." Paul looked from me to Achilles, and a smile spread his lips. "Hey, Achilles. How are you?"

"I'm good. It's nice to see you looking so healthy, Paul," Achilles commented.

I sat down and motioned to the ground. "Come sit, Paul. I wanted to catch you up."

"Well, if it has to do with why you look so happy, I'm all for it." Paul sat down and moved his book to the side.

"I see you got wrangled into reading the assassin werewolves, too?" I motioned to the book.

"I'm already on book five!" Paul exclaimed. "They are really good!"

"I know. I have a huge crush on Mateo," I admitted.

"Wow, so you too, huh?" Paul stared at me.

A huge sigh came from above us and we both looked at Achilles.

"I guess I'll have to read them now as well." He grinned.

"Paul, I want to tell you myself that Achilles and I are together now." I wrapped an arm around Paul's shoulders. "He confronted my parents, and it turns out Holden wrote me a goodbye letter leaving me his motorcycle."

"I knew it!" Paul blurted. "I'm so sorry you had to go through all that, Harley."

"Well, it made me stronger. I went to Holden's grave and lost my shit."

"Good." Paul nodded. "You needed to grieve." Paul stared up at Achilles with a grin. "So, you finally got your man. Does he know how you found him all those times he disappeared?"

"Wait, what?" I glared at Achilles.

"Your watch and phone are equipped with GPS devices," Achilles winked.

"Sonofabitch! I thought you were just really good." I cursed.

"Oh. I am." Achilles wiggled his brows.

"Yep. You two are meant for each other," Paul laughed.

"I can't wait until you come home, Paul. We really miss you." I hugged him to me.

"Well, I needed time to heal. You know Gareth calls, writes, and comes to see me? After everything I did to him, he still watches out for me. He forgave me for everything." Paul shook his head sadly.

"PTSD and clinical depression are serious, Paul," Achilles spoke up. "The guys were right to put you in here. Your doctor says you're coming along quite nicely."

"Well, I look forward to the day that I can be back in my house and be a part of your lives."

"You'll always be a part of our lives, Paul; you're family."

Paul and I sat around, chatting about the books and the band. Achilles was over at the bench on his phone, and Paul ribbed me. I glanced over at him to see a huge smile on his face.

"I knew he wanted you, he pretty much said it last time you guys were here," Paul admitted.

"He's such an awesome man." I sighed, staring at Achilles dreamily.

"I'm happy for you, Harley. I knew some day the right person would come along and see you."

"Thanks, Paul."

~*~

The halls were crowded with fans as Achilles and I entered the hotel. I stopped and signed quite a few autographs while Achilles kept a lookout. The rest of the guys were filing in and I caught sight of Jinx with Jayden and his boys. I waved and Jinx winked as he and Jayden crossed the lobby to us. A scream filled the air and Achilles moved in front of me instinctively. I peered around him to see Evander Torrin pinned to a wall by a crazed fan. Achilles made to move, but in a flash, a huge body ripped the crazed fan off of Evander and held him firm.

"Back it off!" Hammer shouted.

I stood transfixed to the spot as Hammer assessed Evander from head to toe. He said something to the young man, who just nodded, eyes wide, before he stepped back and put a hand out, indicating that Evander should keep walking. Hammer held onto the fan as Evander left, throwing glances over his shoulder as he did. I pulled on Achilles' shirtsleeve and he looked down at me with a grin.

"Seems our bodyguard is guarding a new body." I winked.

"Well, Marc doesn't talk about his love life, so who knows?" Achilles took my hand.

We filed into the studio and I sidled up to Evander, elbowing him in the ribs.

"What was that all about?" I asked.

"I have no idea where that fan came from. He tried to grab my dick." Evander stared at me with huge eyes.

"You're so cute, all British." I wrapped an arm around him.

"Ugh."

Sebastian floated into the room with a folder in his hand and flopped into his director chair. He flipped the folder open and then assessed us all.

"We are sold out, gentlemen. Not only have you all agreed to be here, but Sal Falco has come on as master of ceremonies. I don't have to tell you how fortunate I am that you all signed on for this, so I owe you all a huge debt of gratitude. You have today to rehearse and we go live tomorrow. I wish you all the best and thank you all for doing this."

"Not a problem, Sebastian. You know me and the guys would do anything for you," Jayden said.

"Any chance you and Jinx could do another song together?" Sebastian grinned like a Cheshire cat.

"We'll all be out onstage together and we're already singing side by side," Jayden reminded him.

"I had to ask." Sebastian stood, righted his slacks, and then shot us a half wave. "Have fun."

I immediately sought out Ransom and grinned at the look of shock on his face. Ransom seriously had the hots for Sal Falco and, right about then, he was shitting himself. I crossed the room to him and flung an arm around his shoulders.

"Sooo." I eyed my fingernails casually. "Sal Falco, huh?"

"Don't start. I'm nervous enough as it is." Ransom ran his hands through his hair.

"We'll be great! We always are. Now, let's get to rehearsals."

~*~

All of us together on one stage was actually pretty comical. We all had different ways of doing things, so coming together and making it work? Not an easy feat. I was sandwiched between Dante from Black Ice and Wheland from Ivory Tower. Not a bad sandwich, if you asked me. Ransom was out front with Dagger and Zander. Gareth was on the other side of the stage with Lincoln and Jared. Cooper and Ashton, along with Jayden, were on drums and Jinx was out front with Tony on piano. I had a great view of Achilles in the front row, and halfway through "November Rain" he gave me a thumbs up. Evander and the Spiros twins were singing backup and we'd have an orchestra behind us tomorrow night for the live show.

We practiced all three songs, and when we were done, Sebastian walked onto the stage clapping.

"Wonderful! I shall see you all tomorrow night. Relax tonight and have some fun."

I shot down the stairs and jumped on Achilles, wrapping around him like a boa constrictor.

"Was it good?" I asked.

"Perfect."

Lights came up on the two grand pianos, illuminating Jinx and Tony. The crowd was up and clapping immediately. Jayden, along with Cooper and Ashton, came in with the drums. The orchestra began its swell and the entire arena was filled with whistles and clapping. Ransom began to sing first and then the rest of us blended in. As always, I had a perfect view of Achilles in the front row, and I smiled when our eyes met. Gareth was like a kid in a candy store and I understood why. We were doing this for LGBT youth, kids who'd been kicked out for their sexuality and had nowhere else to go.

Our band, as well as Ivory Tower, Black Ice and London Boys, had contributed a million dollars to the charity already, but the kicker? Sal Falco had pledged a million dollars all by himself. I spared a glance at Ransom, who was rocking it out on the stage, and then zeroed in on Sal off to the side. He was watching Ransom's every move. I didn't know if he'd pledged just to get in good with Ransom, and I didn't care. That money was going toward a good cause.

The crowd went crazy as Gareth got up on top of the piano with Dante and Wheland, banging out the guitar portion of the song. The whole place stood up as we launched into the final part of the song. All of us were banging our heads, jumping around on stage as we pumped out the song across the filled aisles. The lights went down and the place broke out in pandemonium. They came back up and we all formed a line, bowing together.

"Put your hands together for these guys!" Sal shouted into the mic. "Get ready for the next song, and make sure you call the number at the bottom of your screen. Let's show these kids they are not forgotten!"

The music began for "Damn, I Wish I Was Your Lover" and I mouthed the words to Achilles in the front row, who just laughed. Jayden and Evander crossed back and forth, singing the song as the rest of us backed them up. Ransom came in on the second verse and once again, the crowd was up on their feet whistling. The three of them began singing together and pointing into the audience. I couldn't stop laughing, it was one of the best times of my life. We all played a few songs from our last albums before we headed off to change for the final number.

We wrapped it up with Tesla's "Love Song" and Gareth and the other guitar players sat on stools playing the intro. They were perfectly in sync; it was awesome. The winner from *Singers*, Jericho, sang with Zeke, his runner-up and now part of his band. The crowd was up on their feet again and singing along. Ransom joined in, along with Dagger and Zander, and they all took the stairs down to the audience, shaking hands with the crowd. I moved to the side with the other guitar players as we finished up the song to a screaming arena. We all bowed and the lights went down on us. The curtain closed and I wiped at my forehead.

"Holy shit!" Gareth yelled. "That was awesome!"

"We now have two hours of VIP ticket holders," I reminded him.

"Love it!"

The next two hours were spent taking pictures with fans and signing autographs. Gareth always loved this part, meeting fans and hearing how our music and lives had changed them in some small way. I stood next to Achilles as a reporter from *Hollywood Now* interviewed me.

"So, Harley, tell us about the man at your side." She shoved the microphone in my face.

"Well, this is Achilles Castellanos, my bodyguard and boyfriend."

"Wow, didn't see that one coming." She laughed. "Is the whole band gay?"

"You never know." I winked.

"Well, he is definitely big enough to guard your body," she leered.

"You have no idea." I leered right back.

"Oh! I see Jinx and Jayden, gotta run! Kisses!" she called out as she scrambled to catch Jinx.

"Well, that was …fun." Achilles cocked a brow.

"Are you okay with me introducing you as my boyfriend?" I asked.

"More than okay. I am, right?"

I nodded.

"Well, there ya go." Achilles took my hand and laced our fingers together. "What's next?"

"More pictures with the bands, and interviews."

"Let's get to it then."

~*~

We ended up at Sebastian's Hollywood Hills home for the after party. The house was filled to the rafters as we all hung out and talked about the show. One of the best things about being in my position was that I could reach out to those in trouble and help them. I watched Achilles across the room talking to Axel and Buster. He was so full of life and my heart ached for everything he'd been through. He truly was a survivor.

"Hey."

I glanced over my shoulder to see Ransom and Gareth behind me. Both of them were sporting huge smiles.

"Hey, guys. What's up?" I asked.

"Gareth and I just wanted to say how happy we are for you. You got one hell of a good man."

Achilles looked over his shoulder and our eyes met. He smiled at me and I grinned back.

"Yeah. Yeah, I did. So what's up, Ransom? Sal didn't make it to the after party?"

"Said he was busy." Ransom shrugged.

I narrowed my eyes and Ransom fidgeted. "You're hurt."

"Nah, it's all good. He's a busy guy, ya know? Just because he emailed me a few times doesn't mean we're besties."

"What's up with Hammer?" Gareth nodded to the corner where Hammer was standing regulation military style.

"I don't know. He went ape shit when that fan touched Evander," I answered.

"Hmm." Gareth's brows furrowed. "I wonder…"

"Don't start playing matchmaker, Gareth," Ransom warned.

"But I'm so good at it!" Gareth snickered.

"He really is," I agreed.

"Now we just need to find Ransom and Rebel someone." Gareth beamed at his brother.

"I think Rebel's love just walked in." I pointed to the door and Ransom and Gareth turned around. Stan walked in and cast a look around before waving to us and crossing the room.

"Stan and Rebel?" Ransom's brows knit in confusion. "I don't see it."

"Ohh! This could be fun!" Gareth rubbed his hands together in glee.

"Stop it, Munchkin." Ransom mussed Gareth's hair.

"Hey guys!" Stan said excitedly. "Sorry I'm late. I stopped in to see Paul."

"Good to have you here, Stan," I said, wrapping an arm around his shoulders.

"What did I miss?" Stan asked.

"Gareth playing matchmaker," Ransom scoffed.

"Yeah? Who he's setting up this time?" Stan regarded all of us.

"You don't want to know. Let's get a drink, Stan." I pulled him away from Ransom and Gareth, and shot a look at Gareth, who was wiggling his brows.

The rest of the evening I spent right next to Achilles. He and the other bodyguards were talking with Sebastian about putting a detail on the London Boys. They had security at concerts, but not a full-time staff. I pulled Achilles away and pushed him into a corner, attacking his mouth. Achilles wrapped his arms around me, pulling me flush with his body, and my dick felt like an iron rod in my jeans. Achilles broke the kiss panting, and he stared into my eyes.

"Are you ready to go?"

"Are you?"

Achilles took my hand and we practically ran through the house, saying our goodbyes on our way out. We caught a limo out front and Achilles opened the door for me. We settled in and Achilles put the partition up. I leaned back in the seat and spread my legs open wide with a salacious grin on my face.

"Why, Mr. Castellanos, what are you up to?" I licked my lips.

"About nine inches."

Achilles grabbed my thighs and yanked me to my back on the seat. Seconds later, he was devouring my mouth like a man possessed. My hands were pinned above my head and Achilles had his other hand down my pants. I arched into his touch and a loud moan left me and rumbled into Achilles' mouth.

"Fuck," Achilles rasped. "Want you."

"How long until we get to the hotel?" I asked, pumping my hips into him.

"Stop that," Achilles warned.

"Or?" I gripped the hair on his nape and yanked him back to my mouth.

"I'm going to fuck you in this limo." Achilles ground into me. "I want you in a bed."

"Five minutes." I held up my fingers. "Hang on for five minutes."

When the limo pulled up in front of the hotel, Achilles flew out the door, dragging me with him. We boarded the elevator and Achilles paced as it ascended.

"Just watching you, I'd never peg you as a bottom," I observed.

Achilles stopped pacing and leveled a glare at me. "I said I like being a bottom, I never said I wouldn't top; and right now, I want to fuck you six ways from Sunday."

"Can this thing go any faster?"

Achilles broke out into a huge grin and grabbed me as the doors opened. We made it to the room and Achilles wasted no time opening it. The door slammed against the wall and Achilles shoved me up against it, taking my mouth in a ferocious kiss. I fumbled with his jeans as he practically ripped mine off. I wrapped my arms around his neck as he lifted me, pinning me to the door as he ravished every inch he could reach.

I could barely breathe and I fucking loved it.

Achilles gripped my ass cheeks and took me to the bedroom. He dropped me on the bed and yanked my boxers down. I watched him intently as he grabbed lube and gripped his dick, making sure he stroked it in full view.

"Get on your hands and knees. Ass in the air," Achilles commanded.

I actually shivered at his tone of voice and quickly did as he ordered. I peered over my shoulder to see Achilles crawling onto the bed ever so slowly, his eyes perusing my naked backside. His features were stoic, as if he was calculating his next move. I couldn't wait. His hand landed on my ass and I moaned from the sting of his palm. Achilles bent in, licking one cheek and then the other.

My legs spread out a little more, and then Achilles' nose was buried in my ass. I let out a yelp of surprise as Achilles tongued my asshole. His fingers dug into my flesh and I squeezed my eyes shut and bit my bottom lip to keep from crying out. The room began to swim as Achilles tortured me relentlessly and just when I thought I couldn't take it anymore, he slid an arm under my waist and flipped me to my back.

"Holy shit," I rasped.

Achilles' eyes were black as night from desire and I couldn't wait for him to fuck me.

My mouth watered and I grabbed his biceps as he lifted me into his arms, kissing me again. I locked my legs around his hips as we continued to kiss frantically. I wanted him to fuck me up against the wall; I was so damn horny. Achilles stood, taking me with him as we fumbled around the room, both of us knocking shit over.

Achilles broke from the kiss gasping and I helped him to get his shirt off. His skin was hot and I ran my hands over his pectoral muscles. My back hit the wall and I moaned out loud as Achilles bit my shoulder.

"Fuck, yes!" I practically shouted.

Heat tore up my back and I cried out as Achilles sunk his dick into my ass. My fingers broke the skin on his shoulders as he stopped halfway in.

"Fuck, I shouldn't have done that," Achilles started.

"Keep going, fucking burns like a mother fucker, but feels so damn good."

"I should have —"

"Shut up."

I began to move up and down on Achilles' dick. As my body stretched to accommodate him, the pleasure came and I closed my eyes in bliss. Every thrust slammed my back against the wall, and damn if that didn't turn me on even more. I sucked on his neck, leaving a dark mark. He was mine and I felt it in every fiber of my being.

Our tongues slid against each other, and the thrusting became more erratic as we neared orgasm. I held on and moved with him as his hips thrust harder and harder into me; my whole body screamed for release. And when it came, I was shouting through it, my cum blasting up Achilles' chest. Achilles shuddered, and then molten heat shot through my body. My head fell back against the wall and Achilles kissed along the corded muscles of my throat.

"Damn." I let my head fall forward and looked into the worried eyes of Achilles. "What's wrong?"

"Did I hurt you?"

"Hell, no. I mean, I'm sore, but I fucking loved it!"

Achilles kissed me and gently lowered me to the floor. We got to the bed and I turned onto my back, staring at the ceiling with what I knew was a shit-eating grin.

"Ready to go home tomorrow?"

"Yes. I am. I want to get a Christmas tree."

"So we will." Achilles traced the hair around my belly button with his fingertip. "You sure you're okay?"

"Hell, yes. Damn, I love it when you get all forceful and demanding. It's so hot!"

Achilles chuckled and bent over to lick my stomach. "You taste good."

"I didn't clean up."

"I can do it."

My fingers played in his hair as Achilles licked me clean. He kissed up my chest until our lips met.

"You're going to have the best Christmas ever, Harley. I promise."

Chapter 21

Harley

As soon as we got back to town, I went to see Arielle-Adrianna. She'd fucked up royally, but I felt she needed to know why I'd broken up with her so long ago. I stopped by her father's house, and he informed me that she was in the hospital undergoing detox. She'd made bail apparently. I checked in at the front desk at the hospital and told them who I was. A nurse ushered me to Adrianna's room and I closed the door behind me. She looked so small, so frail; and in that moment, I actually felt sorry for her.

"Hey," I said, as I moved a chair over to the side of her bed.

"Harley?" Adrianna croaked. "What are you doing here?"

"I felt like you needed to hear why I did what I did so long ago."

"You don't owe me anything after what I did." Adrianna closed her eyes.

"I kinda do. See, when we were dating, I knew at some point you'd want to come to my house and meet my parents. I couldn't let that happen. You have no idea what my life was like back then — hell, what it's been like over the past three years. Back then, it was as if I wasn't even there, and it only got worse over time. I wasn't ashamed of you, Adrianna. I was ashamed of *me*."

"What?" She opened her eyes at that.

"I am invisible to my parents, I always have been. I didn't want you to see that. As for my love life now? Well, let's just say I didn't think I'd fall for a man, but here I am."

"I'm so sorry, Harley," Adrianna whispered.

"Well, you didn't kill us, that's a plus, right?" I tried to grin.

"Stop that. Don't make this into some kind of joke. I know what I did, and I know I belong in jail for it. Hell, maybe it will help me get clean."

"When did you…well, you know?"

"In my first year of acting. I was so tired all the time and one of the guys offered me a pick-me-up. I didn't know what it was at the time, so I stupidly took it. Then I got busted with a friend for having weed and it just escalated from there. Now I'm in hell and I know I belong here."

I patted her hand and leaned in, giving her a smile. "You'll kick it. You're a strong person, Adrianna."

"Is…your boyfriend okay? He kind of scared the ever-living shit out of me. I left him up there…" Adrianna trailed off.

"He's fine. Achilles is one hell of a man, Adrianna."

"He really is. Thank you, Harley. For coming to see me."

"You bet."

~*~

I spent my Christmas Eve birthday with the guys. They took me out to dinner and showered me with gifts. Okay, sex toys, but it was the thought that counts. I sat with Jinx as Achilles and the other bodyguards stood around talking. Jinx was watching Jayden across the room with the rest of the London Boys. Gareth plopped down into the chair next to me, and Ransom and Rebel took the seats across from me. We all sat there staring at each other for the longest time before Rebel spoke.

"So. Thirty-one, eh? It's all down hill from here, bud."

"You'll all be catching up to me real soon. Well, except for Gareth." I winked.

"I think I speak for all of us when I say Achilles is the best thing to ever happen to you." Ransom took my hands across the table. "Any word from your parents?"

"Nope. Not even today, of all days. They didn't even call to ask if I was going to follow through on Achilles' threat."

"Are you?" Jinx asked.

"I don't know. They are still my parents, you know? Besides, I have all the love I could want from you guys." I wiggled my brows.

"Well, we expect to see you and Achilles at my parents' house for Christmas," Jinx cut in. "You know how much my mom loves you."

"I'll be there with my gramps." Rebel grinned.

"Oh hell," Ransom sighed. "Will you make sure he stays dressed this time?"

"Why? I thought him chasing you while waggling his dick was pretty comical," Rebel snickered.

"That is, like, burned on my temporal lobe," Gareth groaned.

"Hey, my gramps says life is too short to play by the rules."

"Didn't that get him banned from the book store?" Ransom chortled.

"What is Achilles up to over there? He seems very preoccupied on his phone." Jinx tilted his head, watching Achilles.

"I don't know," I shrugged. "Said he had a surprise for me when I got home."

"You two are so cute together," Gareth mused. "I could tell he liked you from the beginning."

"Oh? So now you know everything, little matchmaker?" I mussed Gareth's hair.

"The day they walked into the dressing room, I saw Achilles' face the second he laid eyes on you." Gareth pointed at me. "It was all over his face."

"Yeah, well, he's everything to me," I said, staring at Achilles dreamily.

"Three down, two to go!" Gareth eyed Ransom and Rebel.

"Now wait." Rebel lifted a hand. "I don't think there's anyone out there who can put up with my shit."

"Yeah?" Gareth sat forward and pinned Rebel with a look. "I think there is."

"Hey guys!" Stan walked over to our table and sat down in the chair next to Rebel. "Happy birthday, Harley. What did I miss?"

We all laughed as Rebel stared at Stan.

"Uh huh." I leaned back, crossing my arms.

"We were just talking about Rebel's gramps," Jinx hurriedly spoke.

"I love that guy! He cracks me up." Stan laughed, wiping at his eyes. "He bought me an inflatable doll for my birthday."

"He did?" Rebel asked in astonishment.

"Yep, but it was a woman doll, so I had to explain. He just taped a cucumber on it." Stan cracked up.

"Oh God." Rebel banged his head on the table.

"He wanted to know if he could go with me to the gay club," Stan admitted.

"What?!" Rebel lifted his head.

"Yep," Stan nodded. "Wanted to be my wing man."

"Oh Jesus," Rebel whispered. "I'm so sorry."

"Don't be! We had a blast," Stan replied.

"You mean he actually went?" My mouth dropped open.

"Yep. He regaled all the guys with his war stories. I think he has a boyfriend now." Stan chuckled.

"I can't leave that man for two seconds." Rebel sighed.

"Oh, so anyway, Harley, Sal Falco gave us all tickets to the movie premiere and he says happy birthday."

"Awesome." I turned to Ransom. "Will you be attending?"

"Shut up," Ransom grumbled.

"Happy birthday, Harley," the guys all sang in unison.

"Thanks, guys."

I caught Achilles' eyes from across the room and he grinned at me salaciously. I couldn't wait to get him home.

~*~

I stood looking at the ginormous tree in my living room with my mouth agape. When I said a tree, I meant like a five footer, or something like that. This tree touched the ceiling and ornaments of all kinds hung from its branches. Achilles really loved Christmas, I guess. I hadn't really thought about it too much over the years. After Holden died, I'd stopped celebrating all together. Now I had a life with Achilles and I wanted to celebrate everything I had.

"Wow!" I gushed.

"Wait until I turn on the lights!" Achilles said excitedly.

"You look like a little kid." I grinned at him.

"It's too much, huh?" Achilles frowned up at the tree.

"No. I really do love it. I love the ornaments, too. We'll have to call your mom and dad and thank them for all this."

"They love you, Harley." Achilles crossed the room to me and took my hand. He pulled me over to the tree and pointed out one of the ornaments. "Look at this one. It's you in front of the temple."

"I don't remember wearing a Santa hat." I smiled.

"Photoshop. My mom loves doing stuff like that."

"Well? Put the lights on." I pushed him playfully.

Achilles went behind the tree and I turned off all the lights in the living room. Achilles plugged them in and I stood in awe in front of the tree. Multi-colored lights painted my walls in a rainbow of colors as they twinkled on and off.

"There's an ornament for Holden, too." Achilles pointed to it and I leaned in. It was Holden and me on his bike. We were both smiling.

"I love it," I whispered, tears in my eyes.

"So, Christmas is tomorrow. Anything you really want?" Achilles asked.

I looked over at him. "I have everything I could possibly want."

We sat in front of the tree and watched the lights for what seemed like hours, both of us talking about past Christmases while sipping hot cocoa. I leaned against Achilles' shoulder as the lights flickered on and off. I smiled and thought of Holden and how much he loved Christmas.

"Ready for bed?" Achilles stood and then helped me to my feet.

"I am," I yawned.

"Good. Get some sleep. I have a surprise for you later."

~*~

I woke up to the bed dipping, and rolled over to find Achilles hovering above me with a huge grin. I wiped the sleep from my eyes and smiled up at him.

"What time is it?" I asked sleepily.

"It's eleven fifty-five. Come with me." Achilles took my hand.

I got up and walked with him. The Christmas tree lights were blinking as we passed through the living room. Achilles stopped in front of the garage door and checked his watch.

"What are you doing?"

"Shh." Achilles lifted my face to his and kissed me lightly. He pulled away slowly and palmed my cheek. Checking his watch once more, Achilles placed my hand on the knob of the door.

"Happy birthday, Harley," Achilles whispered.

I twisted it and walked into the brightly lit garage. Snowflake lights hung down, bathing the garage in white light, and in the center of it all was Holden's motorcycle. I covered my gasp with my hand as I took in the bike. It was as if it had never been in an accident. I approached it slowly, for fear it would disappear if I got too close. I touched it with a shaky hand and tears began to flow down my cheeks. It was so beautiful. Holden's name was painted along the side of the tank in beautiful red and orange paint with his birthdate and the date of his death. I turned to Achilles, not able to speak. He simply took my hand and pulled me into his arms.

"Merry Christmas, Harley."

"This is…it's so beautiful, Achilles!"

"It's all yours, Harley, just like she should have always been. Holden wanted you to have her."

"I have something for you, too." I took another long look at the incredible gift and led him back into the house and sat him on the couch.

I grabbed the present for Achilles from its hiding spot behind the tree and handed it to him. Achilles eyed it and then turned to me.

"You didn't have to get me anything."

"Just open it."

I watched as Achilles carefully opened his present, making sure not rip the colorful Christmas paper. He pulled open one side and peered inside. His head snapped up and I took his hand.

"You're my lobster, Achilles," I said quietly.

Achilles removed the stuffed lobster and held it up. He noticed the lobster keychain hanging from the side and grinned, removing it.

"I'll put this on my keychain right away." Achilles put the present down and took my face in his hands. "You are *my* lobster, Harley Payne."

Achilles kissed me and I practically melted right into him. We broke from the kiss and I peered at him through my lashes.

"There's something else in there."

"There is?" Achilles lifted the paper and held it upside down. The ornament I'd had made slipped into his hand. Two lobsters were holding claws and underneath in cursive it said, "Harley and Achilles, Christmas 2015".

"I love it." Achilles stood and hung the ornament on the tree.

"I have to tell you something."

"Okay." Achilles came back to the couch and sat down, leaning back on the cushion.

"I, um, don't have a motorcycle license."

Achilles grinned, and then a loud laugh escaped him. He took my hands.

"You'll get one."

I made love to Achilles until well into the morning hours. I couldn't get enough of him. Besides, it was my birthday.

~*~

We arrived at the Jett house a little late, but Jinx's mom forgave me. Then she put me to work. I helped her stuff the turkey while Jinx made more stuffing. Pecan and pumpkin pie scents wafted through the whole house. I wiped flour from my forehead and yelped when someone pinched my ass. I turned to find Achilles grinning widely.

"Hey sexy," he rumbled huskily.

"Hi." I blinked up at him. He was so gorgeous in his black turtleneck sweater. He had to wear it because I'd sucked on his neck like a vamp all night. The thought made me chuckle and Achilles bent down, kissing my forehead.

"Are you almost done in here?" he asked.

"You can't rush greatness," I said, planting my hands on my hips.

"That's right, now shoo!" Jinx's mom swatted Achilles' bicep and he left the kitchen. She turned to me and wrapped me in her arms. "I am so happy for you! You have a wonderful man at your side."

"Thank you," I said. "That I do."

She pulled away and palmed my cheek. "You are very special, Harley Payne. You are like another son to me. Merry Christmas and happy birthday."

"It was yesterday." I smiled.

"I know that. I have an extra present under the tree for you."

"You didn't have to do that."

"Oh, I know." She winked.

Once the cooking duties were over, I wandered into the living room and Achilles pulled me into his lap. I snuggled in and we watched a football game together. The guys were very vocal about their team and I just smiled at all of them. I felt as if I were at home, as if I finally had a place to be where I fit in. Jinx's mom called us all to the table and there was a groan from all the guys.

"You can watch the game from the table, ya big babies!" she laughed.

We moved to the large table filled with food and I was seated between Achilles and Jinx. I bowed my head as Jinx's mother said a prayer.

"I want you all to say something you're thankful for!" She pointed at all of us.

"I'll start," I blurted out. I took a look around the table and smiled. "I'm so thankful that you all put up with me —"

Laughter filtered across the room and I sobered.

"I'm so lucky to have all of you. You treat me like family, and I am so grateful to all of you. Thank you so much for all that you do."

"You're like my son, Harley." Jinx's father mussed my hair. "We love you."

Achilles held my hand as the others said what they were thankful for. It finally got to him, and Achilles glanced over at me with a small smile.

"I am so thankful I said yes to Mac the day he called and asked me to work for him. Otherwise, I would have never found the love of my life. My lobster." Achilles kissed my forehead.

"Awww!" they all said in unison.

"Merry Christmas!" Jinx's mom lifted her glass.

"Merry Christmas!"

~*~

I was half asleep in Achilles' lap from turkey overload when Jinx's mom placed a present in my hand. I looked up at her with a grin.

"Thank you for my electric mixer, Harley. How did you know I needed one?" she asked.

I pointed to Jinx and he stuck his tongue out at me.

"Well, I love it." She bent down and kissed my cheek. "Open yours."

I unwrapped it carefully and smiled. "It's so beautiful."

It was an ornament. The picture inside was of all of us together and at the bottom in glitter was the word "family".

"Thank you so much," I whispered.

"We love you, Harley." Jinx's mom smiled.

I sat staring at the ornament in my hand as Jinx's mom moved off to hand out more gifts. Achilles leaned into my ear.

"Merry Christmas, Harley."

"Merry Christmas."

Chapter 22
Harley

I felt free as I left the DMV. I'd spent the last three days testing for my motorcycle license and I'd finally gotten it. I rode Holden's bike home and let the chilly air sweep across my face. My life with Achilles was just beginning and I'd never been so happy. He'd been busy the last couple days working with Axel and Mac training new recruits. I'd seen a few of them; they were just like the others — tall and scary.

I pulled into the driveway and the garage door lifted slowly, revealing Achilles' Tomahawk parked off to the side and his pick-up truck parked next to mine. I slid the bike in between them and shut off the engine. I climbed off and set the helmet on the seat. I could hear music in the house and entered, throwing my keys into the bowl by the back door. I wandered through the house, listening for where the music was coming from. As I entered the kitchen, I found Achilles seated at the table with a cake.

"Look what I got!" I held up my license.

"I knew you could do it!" Achilles bounded off the chair and enveloped me in a hug.

"What's all this?" I asked as he let me go.

"I knew you'd pass, so I made you a cake." Achilles pulled out a chair for me and I sat down. The round cake was blue with white letters that spelled out, "Congrats on passing, Harley!"

I looked up at Achilles and tears formed in my eyes. It had to have been the sweetest thing he'd done for me besides fixing Holden's bike. Achilles sat down and took my hand.

"Is this okay? I thought since Holden used to do it for you —"

"I love it, Achilles. Thank you so much," I said, a smile lifting my lips. "This is very sweet of you."

"If you'd failed, I still would have made you a cupcake." Achilles grinned.

And that right there was what I loved most about Achilles. Was he a badass? Yep. Could he kill someone from a mile away? Yep. He could also love and make me feel like the most important person on the planet.

"I'm going to eat this cake off your ass," I said huskily.

"Well, let's go then."

~*~

Seeing Achilles buck-naked on his hands and knees on my bed, ass hiked up in the air, was the best present I could ever get. I licked my lips and swiped some frosting off the cake. I set the cake off to the side and crawled up on the bed. I slapped Achilles' ass, spreading icing all along his ass cheek. Achilles groaned and dropped his head.

"Grab your dick and jack off," I ordered as I moved over him.

Achilles did as I commanded, and I slipped my fingers down his crease, coating it with icing. There was a loud intake of breath from Achilles and then I bent over, swiping at his ass with my tongue. As much as I loved forceful Achilles, I also loved hearing him whimper and moan at my touch.

"Fuck, you're even better than the cake," I groaned against his skin.

I loved seeing his fingers grasping at the blanket, the way his ass pushed back into my face, begging for more. But the best part was hearing him when I finally sunk inside him. I bent my knees and grabbed his hips, plowing into him. Achilles made a choked sound and then began to stroke his cock furiously.

"You going to come?" I smacked his ass.

"Yes!" Achilles rasped.

"Do it. Let me hear you."

I nailed his spot relentlessly until Achilles came apart beneath me. His loud shout echoed around the room and then I was coming, my fingers buried in his flesh. I slumped over his back, gasping for air as my orgasm ebbed from me. I pulled out slowly and fell to my back on the bed next to him. Achilles rolled into me, pulling me into his chest.

"Damn, Harley," Achilles panted.

"Yeah? Did you like it when I spanked you?" I chuckled.

"Oh, you're so going to get it from me now."

"I can't wait." I wiggled my brows.

Achilles licked my lips and bit the lower one.

"Want to go again?"

"Give me five." I pointed to my dick.

"No. I'm going to fuck you until you can't walk." Achilles rolled me to my back and hovered above me.

"Oooh! Are you going to get rough?"

Achilles leaned down until our lips were barely touching.

"Just a tad."

"I like it."

"You really are something else, Harley Payne."

"I'm yours, though."

"Yes. Yes you are."

The End.

Sneak Peek at Ransom's book

3 months prior, Sebastian Lowery's Hollywood
Hills home.

I should have brought Scarlett with me. What was I
doing here alone? When Sebastian called and invited me to
his house for some Hollywood party, I should have said
no. Scarlett had begged off tonight due to a headache. I
couldn't really blame her. She attended every single
premiere with me as my girlfriend, so taking the night off
from a party was fine by me. I entered Sebastian's house
and looked around for the man of the hour. As I scanned
the room, my eyes caught sight of a man that I'd been
dreaming about for years.

Ransom Fox stood across from me in all his
delicious glory.

"Sal," Sebastian strode up to me and I leaned into
his ear.

"Please tell me you're going to introduce me," I said
quietly.

"I sure am," Sebastian chuckled.

I'd known Sebastian since we were in our teens.
He'd come to America to make it big and I was on a
sitcom that my dad was producing. Sebastian had tried out
for a role and lost it, but we got along great and I
introduced him to my father. That, as they say, was that.
Sebastian began acting in films and eventually turned to
producing. Sebastian curled his fingers around my bicep
and walked me across the room. Ransom looked petrified
to meet me, it seemed. He had that wild, panicked look in
his eyes.

"Ah, Ransom Fox, I would like to introduce you to my dear friend, Sal Falco." Sebastian pushed me closer to Ransom and he seemed to stiffen.

"What a pleasure, Ransom. I love your music," I said smoothly.

"Wait, what?" Ransom stammered.

Sebastian introduced me to Jinx Jett and I shook his hand, but my attention was focused solely on the gorgeous blond in front of me. Jesus, could God have made a more perfect specimen? Ransom Fox was a wet dream.

"Can I offer you a drink, Ransom?" I motioned to the bar.

"Oh, um, I don't really drink." Ransom bit his bottom lip.

Oh fuck me. Damn, he was sexy when he did that.

"Water, maybe?" I asked.

Jinx coughed and pointed to the corner. "I'll just be over there."

"Uh huh." Ransom nodded, his eyes fixed on me.

I held my hand out, indicating we should move towards the bar and Ransom started walking. I fell into step with him and pulled out one of the high backed stools. Ransom jumped up into one and I took the one right next to him.

"So, you, um, like my music?" Ransom fiddled with a napkin, his attention focused on the wooden top of the bar.

"I really do," I admitted. "I've been into metal since I was a kid."

"I loved you on that show *Neighbors*. Your character was hilarious with all the shit he got himself into."

"You watched that?" I asked in astonishment. "That was my very first show."

"The writing was fabulous. I would watch it religiously. Then when that ended, I watched *Park Place.* You were such a bad boy in that." Ransom laughed.

"Well, I was in my late teens, so you know they had to up the angst." I motioned to the waiter and ordered two waters. Ransom's eyes met mine and a blush hit his cheeks. "You could have been an actor with your looks, you know."

"Oh no. I get camera shy and I'm really not all that." Ransom shook his head.

Was he blind? Ransom could have given me a run for my money as a leading man. He was drop dead fine as all fuck.

"You don't give yourself enough credit, Ransom. I'm sure you have women all over you."

"Because I'm a rock star," Ransom pointed out. "None of them would want me if I wasn't who I am now."

I wanted him on the bar, naked and screaming my name. I had to stop looking at him like he was the last cannoli on the plate or I was going to give myself away.

"No one would want me if I was just plain ole' Salvatore Falco."

"Are you kidding me?" Ransom's eyes went wide. "Have you seen—" Ransom clamped his mouth shut and sipped his water.

"Have I seen what?" I leaned in with a grin.

"Your reviews," Ransom blurted. "All the women want you."

I leaned back in the chair and eyed Ransom. He was biting at his bottom lip and I wanted to bite it myself. He was a little shorter than me, lean but defined. His forearm held a smattering of tattoos and I wanted to lick them. I wondered if he had more, and where they were. Ransom cast a glance at me and I smiled.

"I can't stay long, but I was hoping we could continue this discussion at some point?" I asked.

"Sure." Ransom nodded.

"Well, here is my card with my cell phone and email. I hope to hear from you soon, Ransom. Maybe next time you're in town we can have dinner?"

"Oh, um, sure. I'd like that." Ransom's head bounced up and down and I couldn't help the smile that rose to my lips. Ransom Fox was the guy I'd always wanted. Too bad I could never have him.

Chapter one

Ransom

I hated Los Angeles. I really did. You couldn't pay me to live here. I exhaled in frustration as the car in front of me moved two inches. I'd been stuck in this shit for an hour already and it wasn't looking much better up ahead. I should have taken a limo instead of driving myself in this tiny tic-tac of a rental car. My phone beeped and I looked down at it. My heart began to race as I saw Sal Falco's name on the screen. After the LGBT youth fundraiser, I didn't think I'd hear from him. He basically disappeared right after his duties were done. I felt like I'd done something wrong somehow. Did he figure out I had a huge crush on him? I swiped talk and braced myself.

"Hello?"

"Hey, Ransom. I heard you're in town."

"I am, I'm moving Paul to Arizona, so I have to settle things out here."

"Well, if you're free tonight, we could have dinner?"

I swear I was sweating just talking to him. I needed to get my shit together and act like a fucking man for fuck's sake.

"I could do that. I'm not due at the hospital until morning anyway."

"Well, where are you staying? I can pick you up."

"I haven't decided yet, whatever's closest to the hospital."

"I'm actually not that far. You could stay with me."

I choked on my spit and then broke out in a hacking fit.

"Ransom? Are you All right?"

"Yep," I coughed. "Swallowed my water wrong."

Stay with Sal? That was just begging for me to fuck up somehow. I knew I acted like I had my shit together, but when it came to Sal Falco, I was a teenage girl.

"I'll text you my address. If that's okay? You don't have to stay here."

"No, that's fine. Saves me some money."

"Okay, I'll see you when you get here."

"Okay, thanks, Sal."

I hung up before I could say something really stupid. Two seconds later, Sal texted me his address. Luckily for me, the exit I needed was right ahead.

I finally got off the freeway and headed towards Sal's house. Palm trees lined the roads and manicured lawns were everywhere. Tall gates surrounded beautiful houses as I finally took Sal's street. I checked my phone and slowed down, looking at house numbers. I didn't need to because two houses down, Sal was standing out front of his house. I pulled up to the gate and lowered my window as he approached the car.

"How do you fit in there?" Sal peeked into the car. "Does it plug in?" Sal started laughing.

"This is what happens during a holiday weekend. You get the last of the cars on the lot. It was this or a huge gas guzzler."

"Why didn't you just get a limo?"

I lifted a brow and Sal laughed some more.

"Well, come on in." He moved away from the car and I followed the path around to the front of the house. I had to admit, I didn't know what I was expecting, but Sal's house was very low key. Palms and roses covered the entire front of the house and a small waterfall was off to the side, watering lavender. I got out of the car and popped the trunk. I bent in to get my bag and Sal brushed up against me. My whole body reacted and heat pooled in my balls. I righted myself quickly and pulled my bag out, closing the trunk. We walked to the front door and I took a long look around. Sal came to my side and opened the door.

"This is beautiful," I told him.

"Thanks. I like to bring a little bit of Europe to my houses."

We walked into the foyer and I set my bag down on the hardwood flooring. Plants sprung up in every direction I looked and there were paintings of vineyards on the walls.

"You have a gorgeous house," I said.

"It's all thanks to me."

I turned to see a gorgeous redhead in jeans and a ratty T-shirt. Her makeup was flawless, but she was wearing slippers.

"Ransom, I'd like you to meet Scarlett. My girlfriend."

My gut sank at those last two words. Scarlett was breathtaking. I'd seen her before in pictures, but in person she was even more beautiful.

"It's nice to meet you." I stuck my hand out.

"Well, my, my. Ransom Fox," she purred. "You are even more handsome in person."

"Thank you. Pictures don't do you justice, Scarlett," I responded.

"And he's polite." Scarlett lifted her brows at Sal. "Are we keeping him?"

Sal chuckled. "He's just staying here while he gets his friend's affairs in order."

"Well, if you need anything, you just call on Sal there. He'll take care of your every need." Scarlett grinned.

Sal coughed and shot her a look. I tilted my head and observed them. "Where should I take my stuff?"

"It's down that hall, last room on the right," Sal answered.

"Thank you." I said.

"How about dinner? Still up for it?" Sal asked.

"Oh. Maybe you and Scarlett want to go out?"

"Not me, sweetie. I have lines to run. Maybe next time? I'm sure Sal wants you all to himself." Scarlett batted her eyelashes at me. "So good to meet you."

"You as well. I'll just go get settled then?"

Sal nodded and I took off down the hall. That had to be the weirdest conversation yet. I dropped my bag just inside the guest room and peeked around. More pictures of vineyards and a few of Sal's movie posters covered the walls. I walked up to one of them and just stared at it. Sal was just...wow.

"Settling in?"

I jumped in the air at the voice behind me and Sal chortled.

"Sorry," he snickered. "Hungry?"

My stomach chose that moment to growl and I smiled sheepishly. "I guess I am."

"Well, I know this great place not too far from here. They serve Irish food."

"Aren't you Italian?" I asked.

"Yes, but you're not," Sal pointed out.

"We don't have to eat Irish food just because I'm Irish."

"Maybe I like Irish food." Sal cocked a brow.

"Oh really? What's your favorite?"

"I'll find out once we get to the restaurant."

I laughed and Sal blushed. I wanted him right then. He looked so…vulnerable. Why, oh why did I have to be infatuated with a straight man? I raised my eyes to see Sal watching me and the look in his eyes caught me off guard. He coughed, straightened, and backed towards the door. "Yell when you're ready."

"Okay."

Fuck, how the hell was I supposed to keep my thoughts clean when I was going to be around this man for God knows how long? I'd wanted Sal Falco from the second I saw him on TV.

Fuck my life.

Start the ride from the beginning with: A Marked Man; Alaska with Love; By the light of the Moon; Half Moon Rising; Best Laid Plans; For the Love of Caden; The General's Lover; Russian Prey; An Ignited Passion; Reflash; The Red Zone; Irish Wishes; Pleading the Fifth ; Betrayed; Summer of Awakenings; Into the Lyons Den; The Nik of Time and The Littlest Assassin-Shifters; Lessons Learned; Broken Bonds and Forbidden; Dirty Ross; Savage Love and Locke and Key

The 12 Olympians: Justice for Skylar; At Year's End; Lux Ex Tenebris; Strange Addiction and Ryde the Lightning

From Wilde City Publishing: A Betting Man ; A Marrying Man and A Fighting Man; A Working Man and A Healing Man

The Medicine and The Mob; An Eye For an Eye and The Harder they Fall

The Rock Series: FRET and Jinxed
And, Second Time Around and Gabriel's Fall
Join me on my Facebook pages!
https://www.facebook.com/authorsandrine.g.dion
https://www.facebook.com/pages/Official-Sandrine-Gasq-Dion/137320826386776?ref=hl
@Sandrine_GasqD

https://sites.google.com/site/assassinshiftertree/

Made in the USA
Charleston, SC
18 May 2016